KING OF NOTHING

KING OF NOTHING

A Novel

Lampert x Griffin Urban Universe™

First Edition

ISBN: 978-1-969709-20-3 (paperback)

Printed in the United States of America

A NOTE FROM THE PUBLISHER

This is the first novel from Lampert × Griffin Urban Universe™. The imprint is two brothers. One of us is free. One of us is currently incarcerated. The books we publish here will all reckon, in different ways, with what the streets cost.

King of Nothing is not a celebration. We've known boys like D Roc our whole lives. We've buried some of them. The lifestyle this book depicts is real, and it has a real ending, and the ending is in this book. We didn't soften it.

If you came to this book hoping for a story about a man getting away with it—building an empire, beating the cops, dying rich—this isn't that book. The man in this book wins his war. He loses everything else.

We wrote it that way on purpose.

If you're reading this because somebody you love is in the life right now, we hope this finds them in time. If you're reading because somebody you love is already gone, we're sorry. We carry our own.

Thank you for reading.

— *Lampert × Griffin Urban Universe*™

For everyone who made it out.
And everyone who didn't.

"Heavy is the head that wears the crown."

—William Shakespeare

CHAPTER ONE: CROWN HEAVY

The block knew when D Roc stepped out.

118th Street had a pulse, and right now it was beating for him. Summer heat clung to the concrete like a broke nigga on his last twenty. The air tasted like gunpowder memories and Newport smoke, thick enough to choke on if you wasn't from around here. Somewhere down by Frederick Douglass Boulevard, the 2 train rumbled underground, shaking the foundations of buildings that had stood since before Harlem was Harlem.

D Roc leaned against the blacked-out Charger, chrome wheels catching streetlight, bass thumping low enough to rattle ribcages two buildings over. Fresh white tee, fitted cap pulled low, chain tucked—ain't no need to advertise when everybody already knew. The .40 rode comfortable on his hip, hidden but present, like God in the hood—you couldn't see it but you damn sure felt it.

"Yo, that's five hundred you owe me, nigga!" Tone barked at the dice game, palm out like he was collecting rent.

"Man, fuck outta here with that bullshit," Dre shot back, scooping up his bills. "You can't count for shit."

D Roc watched them argue, didn't say nothing. Didn't have to. The corner moved because he let it move. These young boys ate because he fed them. The respect wasn't requested—it was required.

Peezy sat on a milk crate playing lookout, eyes scanning like a security camera that actually worked. Skinny kid, barely nineteen, but loyal as a pit bull and twice as vicious when he needed to be. Behind him, the neon sign of Kennedy Fried Chicken flickered red and yellow, casting shadows that made everybody look guilty.

A woman in fuzzy pink slides shuffled past, baby on her hip, eyes down. She knew better than to see too much. That's how you survived on 118th—see nothing, say nothing, and mind your motherfucking business.

D Roc pulled a Newport from the pack, sparked it, let that menthol hit his lungs. He didn't smoke cigarettes because he liked them. He smoked because out here, you needed something to do with your hands that wasn't pulling a trigger.

A dog barked somewhere down the block, that deep scratchy bark that said it had been breathing smog too long. The streetlights hummed their broken electric song. This was home—grimy, dangerous, and his.

"Roc!" Peezy hissed, suddenly alert. "Honda. Unknown plates."

D Roc's eyes tracked the beat-up Honda creeping down the block like it was lost. Windows too dark for this time of night. Music playing but not loud enough to match the engine. Plates bent like somebody didn't want cameras reading them too easy.

The car rolled past once. Brake lights flickered at the corner. Then it swung back around.

"That's twice," D Roc said, voice low and cold as a morgue drawer.

Tone and Dre stopped arguing. Peezy stood up. All eyes on the Honda as it crept past a second time, slowing down right in front of them.

D Roc's hand drifted to his waist, fingers brushing the grip of the .40. The Honda's passenger window cracked open three inches. Somebody was looking. Somebody was taking notes.

"You lost?" D Roc called out, not moving from the Charger.

The window went back up. The Honda sat there idling for five long seconds—the kind of seconds that decide if somebody's mama gonna be crying at a funeral next week.

Then it pulled off, slow and deliberate, like it was making a point.

"Jersey plates," Peezy said, squinting at the tail lights. "Saw the crack in the right one."

"Jersey niggas always trying to be somebody," Dre muttered, shaking his head.

"They can try," D Roc said, taking another drag. "Trying don't mean shit when you dead."

He made a mental note. Jersey plates. Cracked tail light. Circling his block twice like they was shopping. That wasn't random. That was reconnaissance. That was somebody sizing him up.

And D Roc didn't like being sized up.

"Yo, I'm heading to Manny's," he announced, crushing the Newport under his Timb. "Y'all hold it down. Eyes open. Anybody circle this block again, I want a plate number and a description. And Peezy—"

"Yeah, Roc?"

"You see that Honda again, you call me before you do shit else. Don't be a hero. Dead heroes don't spend money."

Peezy nodded hard, chest puffed like D Roc had just knighted him.

D Roc slid into the Charger, the leather seats still warm from the day's heat. The engine purred to life, that big V8 growl that made niggas move out the way without being asked. He pulled off slow, scanning every corner, every shadow, every parked car. This was chess out here, and he was always three moves ahead.

Manny's strip club smelled like cheap perfume, desperation, and fried chicken wings from the kitchen in the back. The M in the neon sign outside flickered like it had epilepsy. Inside, purple lights made everything look like a bruise.

D Roc moved through the velvet curtain, past the stage where a thick redbone was working the pole like it owed her money. A few corner boys scattered at the bar threw up nods. Respect. Some young cat in the corner nursing a Hennessy looked at him too long, then looked away quick when D Roc met his eyes. Smart.

He found Manny in the back office, sweating through a knockoff Versace shirt, bald head gleaming under the fluorescent lights, gold chain strangling his fat neck. The desk was covered in receipts, empty liquor bottles, and an ashtray that needed to be dumped two days ago.

"Roc! My boy!" Manny jumped up, wiping his forehead with a towel that had seen better days. "Right on time, baby. Right on time."

"Don't 'baby' me. Where the re-up at?"

Manny's smile faltered. "About that—"

"Don't 'about that' me either." D Roc stepped closer. The office suddenly felt smaller. "We had a time. I'm here at the time. Where. The. Product. At."

"Two short," Manny stammered, that towel working overtime on his forehead. "Just two. Supplier got nervous. Some uniforms came sniffing around last week, asking questions—"

"I don't give a fuck about nervous. I give a fuck about my money." D Roc's voice didn't rise. It didn't have to. "You short two, that's ten grand I can't make. Ten grand I can't make means ten grand I gotta explain to people who don't like explanations. You want me explaining to them why you fucked up?"

"I got eight!" Manny said quick, desperate, hands up like D Roc was pointing something at him. "Eight is good, right? Eight is—"

"Eight is short." D Roc pulled up a chair, sat down slow, like he had all the time in the world. "But we gonna make it work. This time."

Manny exhaled like he'd just been paroled. His whole body sagged with relief.

"Next time you short," D Roc continued, lighting another Newport and letting the smoke curl between them, "I'm gonna assume you playing me. You know what I do to niggas who play me?"

Manny swallowed hard. His Adam's apple bobbed like a fishing lure. "Yeah, Roc. I know."

"Good. Now where's my eight at?"

Manny scurried to the closet like a fat roach when the lights come on, pulled out a duffel bag that looked pregnant with product, and dropped it on the desk. D Roc didn't open it. He didn't need to. He could tell by the weight, by the way it hit the desk, by the way Manny was trying not to look at it.

"Word on the street," Manny said, trying to fill the silence, "is that Bishop got Jersey niggas with money trying to muscle in. New faces. New toys. They been asking around about territories, about who moves what."

"Bishop always got something," D Roc said, standing and shouldering the duffel. "That's why he always gonna be a hype man and never the headliner."

"But these Jersey boys got paper, Roc. Real paper. And guns. Military-grade shit."

Manny leaned closer, voice dropping. "Word is they connected. Like really connected. Colombian connected. The kind of people who make Bishop look like a corner boy with a dream."

"Colombians don't care about Harlem."

"They didn't used to. But things changing out here. Bigger players getting interested in smaller territories." Manny mopped his forehead again. "I'm just saying, Roc. Watch your back. This might be bigger than Bishop beefing with you."

"I don't care if they got tanks." D Roc looked Manny dead in the eyes. "I said what I said. Bishop can bring his whole choir, his Jersey friends, and their grandmothers. I'm still God on 118th."

He left Manny drowning in his own sweat and walked back through the club. One of the dancers, a dark-skinned beauty with legs for days, gave him a look that said she'd do anything for the right price. D Roc kept walking. He had business to handle and a woman at home who gave him everything he needed.

Tasha's crib was in the St. Nicholas Houses on 127th—the projects where generations of Harlem had grown up, fought, loved, and died. Third floor, apartment 3C. D Roc let himself in with the key she gave him after the third time he spent the night. The place smelled like cocoa butter, incense, and that special something that was just her.

She was on the couch in boy shorts and a tank top, natural hair out in a cloud around her head, remote in one hand and a half-smoked blunt in the other. Thick in all the right places—curves that made him forget about the streets for a minute.

"Took you long enough," she said without looking at him, eyes still on the TV.

D Roc dropped the duffel by the door, locked the deadbolt and the chain. "Business."

"Business is your side bitch and I'm tired of being second." She finally turned to look at him, brown eyes sharp. "You know what time it is? Do I look like I'm supposed to be waiting up for you like some worried housewife?"

"You ain't never been second." He crossed to the couch, plucked the blunt from her fingers, and took a hit. The weed hit smooth and strong. Good shit. "You just impatient."

"Impatient is waiting for a nigga who smells like smoke and stress." But she was smiling now, that little half-smile that said she wasn't really mad. "You eat?"

"Nah."

"Good. Me neither." She stood up, and even in boy shorts and a tank top she looked like money. "Come shower with me. You smell like the block and Manny's sad-ass club."

D Roc grinned. This was the Tasha he loved—direct, smart, and not afraid to tell him about himself.

The shower was hot enough to burn, steam filling the small bathroom until it felt like they was in their own private cloud. Tasha stood under the spray, water running down her body, and D Roc just watched for a moment. She was beautiful—not just pretty, but beautiful in that way that made him want to do better, be better.

He stepped in behind her, wrapped his arms around her waist, kissed her neck. She leaned back against him, and for a minute they just stood there like that, water washing away the day.

"You gonna tell me what's wrong?" she asked quietly.

"Nothing's wrong."

"Don't lie to me, D. I can feel it on you."

He sighed. She always knew. "Jersey niggas been circling the block. Bishop probably bringing heat."

"So handle it." She turned in his arms, looked up at him with those eyes that saw everything. "You've handled worse. You're D Roc. You don't let nobody take what's yours."

"I know."

"Then act like it." She kissed him, soft at first, then deeper. "But right now, you're here with me. So be here with me."

And he was.

They made love right there in the shower, water pouring over them, steam rising, her nails in his back, his hands everywhere, both of them moving together like they'd done this a thousand times. It was rough and tender at the same time—the way they always were together. When it was done, they stood there breathing hard, holding each other.

"I love you," she whispered against his chest.

"I love you too, baby."

Later, wrapped in towels and sprawled across her bed, they ate Chinese food straight from the containers. D Roc sparked the blunt and offered it to her.

Tasha shook her head. "I'm good tonight."

"Since when you pass on the smoke?"

"Just not feeling it." She shrugged, took the blunt, hit it once—barely inhaling—and passed it back. "Stomach been weird lately."

D Roc didn't think much of it. Stress did that to people.

"You staying tonight?" Tasha asked, rice stuck to her bottom lip. D Roc reached over and wiped it off with his thumb.

"Yeah."

"Good. I need you here." She put down her food, curled up against him. "Not the corner king. Not the man everybody scared of. Just you. Just Darrell."

He kissed the top of her head. Nobody called him Darrell. Nobody except her and his dead mama. "I'm here."

But even as he said it, his phone buzzed. He grabbed it off the nightstand.

Peezy: *Honda came back. Got plates. NJ - JKL 8374. Slowed down, took pictures. Dre followed them to 145th. They meeting with Bishop's people.*

D Roc stared at the message for a long moment. His jaw clenched.

D Roc: *Good work. Fall back. Don't engage. Let them think they slick. Tomorrow we make moves.*

He set the phone down, but Tasha was already looking at him with that look that said she knew.

"The streets calling?"

"Always." He pulled her closer. "But right now, I'm right here."

She settled against him, but they both knew the truth. The streets never stopped calling. They never gave you a break. And tomorrow, blood was probably gonna spill.

But tonight? Tonight he had this. Tonight he had her. Tonight he could pretend he was just a man and not a king.

A king with a crown getting heavier by the day.

A king who was gonna have to defend his throne real soon.

CHAPTER TWO: BLOOD MONEY

Dawn broke over 118th Street like a hangover—slow, ugly, and unavoidable.

D Roc woke up to Tasha's alarm screaming at 6 AM. She had a shift at the hospital doing intake, legitimate money that kept her clean in the system's eyes. She kissed him on the forehead, still half-asleep herself, and stumbled toward the shower.

He laid there for a minute, staring at the ceiling, listening to the water run. His phone was already blowing up. The game never slept, even when you wanted to.

Tone: *Need to move that product. Fiends already calling.*

Dre: *That Honda was back at 5AM. Same spot. Took more pictures.*

Peezy: *I followed them yesterday. They went to Bishop's spot on Lenox. Stayed for an hour.*

D Roc sat up, cracked his neck, and reached for the Newport pack on the nightstand. He sparked one, let that first hit wake him up proper.

Tasha's TV was still on from last night, some morning news show playing low. The anchor was talking about a drug bust in Washington Heights—thirty kilos, Colombian cartel ties suspected. The feds were getting involved. D Roc watched for a second, wondering if Manny's warning about bigger players had more truth to it than he wanted to believe.

Bishop. That nigga was always a problem, but now he was bringing outside muscle into the equation. Jersey boys with money and guns were a different kind of threat. And if they really did have cartel connections like Manny said, this could get ugly fast.

Tasha came out the bathroom in her scrubs, hair pulled back, face fresh. Even in hospital gear she looked good.

"You leaving?" she asked, already knowing the answer.

"Yeah. Got moves to make."

"Always do." She kissed him anyway, tasting like mint toothpaste and promises. "Be safe. I mean it, D. Whatever you doing today, be smart about it."

"I'm always smart."

"You're always lucky. That ain't the same thing." She grabbed her purse, her keys. "I love you. Text me so I know you alive."

"I will."

She left, and the apartment felt emptier. D Roc got dressed—black hoodie, dark jeans, fresh Timbs, chain tucked, .40 on his hip, extra clip in his pocket. He grabbed the duffel bag from yesterday and headed out.

The projects were just waking up. Old heads sitting on stoops with their morning coffee and cigarettes. Kids catching the school bus, backpacks bigger than they were. A crackhead named Smokey stumbled past, eyes yellow and lost, asking for change D Roc didn't give him.

The Charger was where he left it, untouched. Nobody on 118th was stupid enough to fuck with D Roc's car. He tossed the duffel in the trunk and pulled out, headed to the spot.

The trap house on 115th was a two-story brownstone that looked abandoned from the outside. Boarded windows, graffiti on the walls, steps cracked and crumbling. Perfect camouflage. Inside was a different story.

D Roc let himself in through the back door, the one with three deadbolts and a steel plate. The smell hit him first—weed smoke, bleach, and that chemical tang that came from cutting product. Tone and Dre were in the kitchen, scale on the table, baggies spread out like an assembly line.

"Morning," Tone said, not looking up from his work. He was measuring out grams with the precision of a scientist. "We already moved two this morning. Fiends was lined up like it's Black Friday."

D Roc set the duffel on the counter. "That's four we got here, plus the eight from yesterday. We need to move fast before this Jersey shit gets hot."

"What you wanna do about Bishop?" Dre asked, sealing a baggie with the kind of focus that kept them all out of jail.

"I wanna know what the fuck he's planning." D Roc lit another Newport, let the smoke curl toward the stained ceiling. "Peezy said they met at his spot. That means he's coordinating. That means he thinks he can take something from me."

"Can he?" Tone asked, finally looking up. "My mama always said, 'Don't underestimate hungry men.' Jersey boys got that hunger, Roc."

D Roc's face went cold. "What you think?"

"I think anybody can get touched if they ain't careful. Jersey boys got reputation for not playing games."

"So do I." D Roc pulled out his phone. "Set up a meet with Bishop. Neutral ground. I wanna hear what his mouth is saying before I decide what to do with it."

"You sure that's smart?" Dre asked. "Could be a setup."

"Everything's a setup. That's the game." D Roc exhaled smoke. "But I ain't walking in blind. Y'all gonna be strapped and close. Peezy on lookout. Nova with the camera."

"Nova?" Tone raised an eyebrow.

"Yeah. That kid with the photography hustle. Saw him taking pictures at Manny's last week. He's good with a lens and he don't talk." D Roc scrolled through his contacts. "I want everything on film. Bishop says some slick shit, I want proof."

By noon, the meet was set. Marcus Garvey Park, by the benches near the basketball courts. Public enough that nobody would be stupid, private enough that they could talk real.

D Roc pulled up in the Charger, Tone in the passenger seat checking his nine millimeter like it was a prayer book. Dre and Peezy were already there, posted up near the courts pretending to watch a pickup game. Nova was across the street with a telephoto lens that could count Bishop's nose hairs if needed.

Bishop showed up ten minutes late because niggas like him always thought being on time made you look weak. He rolled up in a black Escalade with rims that cost more than most people's rent. Two Jersey boys climbed out with him—both young, both wearing designer everything, both with that look that said they'd never been hungry a day in their lives.

Rich boys playing gangster. The most dangerous kind.

Bishop was older, maybe forty, with salt-and-pepper dreads and a smile that never reached his eyes. Gold rings on every finger, a Cuban link that could choke a horse, and a suit that was trying too hard to look casual.

"D Roc," Bishop said, arms spread like they were old friends. "Good to see you, young brother."

"Cut the brother shit." D Roc stayed by the car, one hand casual near his waist. "You been sending Jersey niggas to scout my block. That's disrespectful."

"Disrespectful?" Bishop laughed, but it sounded fake. "Nah, that's business. I'm expanding. The city's big enough for both of us."

"Not my part of it."

One of the Jersey boys stepped forward, chest puffed up. He had a thin mustache and a scar over his left eye that looked like it came from a bar fight, not a real one. "Yo, you need to watch your tone, young boy. You talking to—"

D Roc's .40 was out so fast the kid didn't finish his sentence. Tone's nine was pointed at the other Jersey boy. Dre and Peezy materialized from the courts, both strapped. Nova kept filming.

The park went quiet. Even the basketball game stopped.

"I ain't talking to them," D Roc said calmly, gun steady. "I'm talking to you, Bishop. So you need to control your pets before they get hurt."

Bishop held up his hands, still smiling, but the smile was tighter now. "Easy, easy. We're all professionals here."

"Then be professional." D Roc didn't lower the gun. "Tell me why you bringing outside niggas to my territory. Tell me why I shouldn't handle this right now."

"Because you're smart." Bishop's voice dropped the fake friendliness. "Look, D. The game is changing. These Jersey boys got connections—real connections. They moving weight I can't touch. They got protection I can't buy. You work with me, we all eat. You go against me, you go against them. And trust me, you don't want that smoke."

"I ain't scared of smoke." D Roc's finger rested on the trigger, comfortable. "I been breathing it my whole life."

"It ain't about scared. It's about smart." Bishop glanced at the Jersey boys, who were frozen like deer in headlights. "They offering me the Upper West. I'm taking it. But I'm willing to split 118th with you. Fifty-fifty. You keep your corners, I get mine. We both make money."

"I don't split nothing that's already mine."

"Then you gonna lose it." Bishop's smile was gone now. "I tried to do this nice. But if you wanna play hardball, we can play. Ask yourself—you really ready for war? You got what, four, five deep? They got thirty. You got local blocks. They got connects from Newark to Philly. You're a king of your little corner. They're an army."

D Roc stared at him for a long moment. The .40 didn't waver. The park held its breath.

Then he lowered the gun. Slowly. "Tell your army I said good luck. They gonna need it."

He got back in the Charger, Tone with him, and pulled off. In the rearview, Bishop was already on his phone, probably calling someone to tell them the meet went bad.

"That was either real smart or real stupid," Tone said.

"We'll find out which one tonight." D Roc lit another Newport. "Get everybody ready. They gonna retaliate fast. Probably tonight, maybe tomorrow. We need to be ready."

"You really think we can take thirty deep?"

"I think we ain't got a choice." D Roc blew smoke out the window. "And I think they don't know who they fucking with."

By the time the sun set, 118th Street was locked down. D Roc had called in every favor, every soldier, every nigga who owed him. The block was armed to the teeth—AKs, nines, .45s, even a shotgun Dre pulled from somewhere. They had lookouts on every corner, eyes on every approach.

Tasha came home from her shift and found D Roc on her couch loading magazines, gun oil on the coffee table, an ashtray overflowing with Newport butts.

"Jesus Christ, D. What's happening?"

"War." He didn't look up. "Bishop chose sides. Now I gotta choose bullets."

"This is crazy." She sat down next to him, but didn't touch him. "You're gonna get yourself killed. Or locked up. Or both."

"Probably." He loaded another round, the click-click-click rhythmic and cold. "But I ain't going out quiet. I ain't letting nobody take what I built."

"What you built?" Her voice cracked. "Baby, you built a drug empire in the hood. That ain't something to die for."

"It's all I got."

"You got me." She grabbed his face, made him look at her. Her eyes were wet. "You got me, D. Don't I count for something?"

He kissed her, hard and desperate, tasting her tears and his own fear. "You count for everything. That's why I gotta do this. You think I can let niggas run me off my own block? Let them disrespect me? The second I show weakness, I'm dead anyway. At least this way I go down swinging."

She kissed him back, pulled him close, and they made love right there on the couch—fast, rough, like it might be the last time. Maybe it would be.

After, they laid tangled together, her head on his chest, his arms around her.

"If you die," she whispered, "I'm gonna kill you myself."

He almost laughed. "I ain't dying tonight."

"Promise?"

He wanted to. He wanted to promise her forever and tomorrows and growing old together. But D Roc didn't make promises he couldn't keep.

"I love you," he said instead. "Remember that."

Midnight came and went. 118th Street was a ghost town—even the fiends knew to stay inside when the air smelled like gunpowder and bad decisions.

Then, at 2:47 AM, the Honda showed up.

Peezy spotted it first. "Yo! Honda! Same one!"

D Roc was up in seconds, .40 in hand. The Honda crept down the block slow, windows down now, and D Roc could see three niggas inside. The passenger had something in his lap. Something long and dark.

"Get down!" D Roc yelled.

The first shots lit up the night like fireworks.

The Honda's passenger unloaded with a MAC-10, bullets spraying wild, hitting cars, windows, brick. D Roc dove behind the Charger, felt rounds ping off the metal. Tone returned fire, his nine barking loud, and one of the Honda's windows exploded.

Dre came from the side with the AK, and that sound was different—deeper, meaner, more final. The Honda's back tire blew out, the car swerved, and the driver tried to punch it but the blown tire made them fishtail.

Peezy ran up with a .45, dumping rounds into the passenger side. The MAC-10 went quiet.

The Honda crashed into a parked car, steam rising from the hood. The driver tried to run but Tone was on him, pistol-whipped him to the ground. The other two were still inside—one dead, one bleeding bad and begging.

D Roc walked up slow, gun still out, and looked at the driver on the ground. Young kid, maybe twenty-two, nose broken from Tone's gun, crying like a bitch.

"Who sent you?" D Roc asked calmly, like they were discussing the weather.

"Bishop—Bishop and Trey—Trey from Newark—"

"Trey who?"

"Trey Williams! He runs Jersey! Please, man, don't kill me, I got a daughter—"

D Roc looked at Tone. Looked at Dre. Looked at Peezy. Then back at the kid.

"You got a daughter but you out here trying to kill me? That's fucked up, my nigga."

"I'm sorry! I'm sorry! I was just following orders!"

"So was Eichmann." D Roc put the gun to the kid's head. The kid pissed himself. D Roc could smell it.

But he didn't pull the trigger.

"Get the fuck outta here," D Roc said, lowering the gun. "Tell Bishop I said next time, send men. Not boys. Now run before I change my mind."

The kid scrambled up and ran, limping, crying, probably never stopping until he hit Jersey.

Sirens wailed in the distance. Cops were coming. They had maybe two minutes.

"Strip the guns, scatter the shells, burn anything with prints," D Roc ordered. "Tone, you and Dre handle the bodies. Peezy, you was home asleep. We all was. Everybody got alibis?"

They scattered like roaches when the lights come on. By the time the cops showed up, 118th Street was quiet again. Just a crashed Honda, some blood on the concrete, and bullet holes in buildings that had seen worse.

D Roc was back at Tasha's, gun cleaned and hidden, when the detectives knocked. He answered the door in his boxers, rubbing his eyes like they'd woken him up.

"Can I help you, officers?"

"There was a shooting on 118th. You know anything about it?"

"I was here all night. Ask my girl." He gestured inside where Tasha stood in a robe, nodding confirmation.

The detectives didn't believe him. But they couldn't prove otherwise.

They left with nothing but suspicion, and D Roc closed the door, locked it, and leaned against it.

"That was close," Tasha whispered.

"It's just beginning," D Roc said. "Bishop's gonna come harder now. So am I."

He went to the window, looked out at the city lights, at the streets that owned him as much as he owned them.

The crown was getting heavier.

The war was just starting.

And somewhere out there, Bishop and his Jersey friends were planning their next move.

But so was D Roc.

CHAPTER THREE: RETALIATION

The streets were talking.

Word spread fast in the hood—faster than cops, faster than ambulances, faster than truth. By sunrise, everybody from the Polo Grounds to the Douglass Houses knew about the shootout on 118th. One Jersey boy dead, another bleeding out in St. Luke's with a collapsed lung, and a third one running back to Newark with a broken nose and a story about the devil named D Roc.

D Roc sat in the trap house kitchen, sleep-deprived and chain-smoking Newports, watching his phone blow up with messages. Outside, he could hear the 125th Street hustle starting up—vendors setting up tables, the M60 bus groaning past, somebody blasting old-school hip-hop from a boombox like it was still 1995. The smell of bacon from the diner down the block mixed with the chemical stink of the product they were cutting. Half of his messages were from people asking if he was good. The other half were people asking if he needed soldiers. Respect came in different flavors, but they all tasted like fear.

"We famous now," Tone said, counting money at the table. Even after a shootout, the product kept moving. Fiends didn't care about beef—they just wanted their fix. "Niggas from three blocks over asking to join up."

"Fame gets you killed," D Roc muttered, crushing his cigarette in an ashtray that was already full. "We need to move smart, not loud."

Dre walked in from the back room, AK slung over his shoulder like a guitar. "Just got word. Bishop put fifty K on your head. Trey Williams matched it. That's a hundred bands for anybody who can bring them proof you dead."

D Roc didn't flinch. He'd expected it. "How many niggas you think gonna try for it?"

"In this economy?" Dre shook his head. "All of them."

Peezy burst through the back door, breathing hard, eyes wild. "Yo! Yo! They hit the spot on 127th! Burned it down! Everything gone!"

D Roc stood up so fast his chair hit the floor. "How much we lose?"

"Three bricks. Twenty K cash. And..." Peezy swallowed hard. "Lil Marcus was there. He didn't make it out."

The room went silent. Lil Marcus was sixteen, skinny kid with asthma who ran packages because he was trying to get his moms out the projects. Good kid. Loyal kid. Dead kid now.

D Roc's jaw clenched so hard his teeth hurt. "They burned him inside?"

Peezy nodded, tears in his eyes. "Fire department said it was arson. Gas poured everywhere. They wanted it to burn hot and fast."

"Motherfuckers." Tone stood up, fists balled. "They burning kids now? That's how Bishop wanna play?"

D Roc walked to the window, stared out at the street that had raised him and ruined him in equal measure. Lil Marcus's mama worked double shifts at a laundromat, washing other people's dirty clothes so her son could have clean ones. Now she'd be washing the one he'd be buried in

"Get everybody together," D Roc said quietly. The quiet was worse than yelling. "Every nigga we got. Every gun. Every bullet. Tonight, we make Bishop wish he never heard my name."

By noon, the crew was assembled in the trap house basement—a concrete tomb that smelled like mildew and weed smoke. Twenty soldiers, all strapped, all ready to die for D Roc or die trying.

Nova was there too, camera around his neck, looking out of place but not scared. Kid had heart. D Roc respected that.

"Y'all know what happened," D Roc said, pacing in front of them like a general addressing troops. "They hit us. They killed a sixteen-year-old kid. They think we gonna roll over. They think we soft."

Murmurs of disagreement rippled through the room. Nobody thought D Roc was soft.

"So here's what we gonna do." D Roc pulled out a hand-drawn map of Harlem, marked with X's and circles. "Bishop got three spots. One on Lenox—that's his main money house. One on 145th—that's where he keeps product. And one on Malcolm X Boulevard—that's where he sleeps."

Tone leaned forward. "We hitting all three?"

"Nah. We hitting Lenox." D Roc tapped the map. "We take his money, we hurt him where it counts. The product spot is too hot—too many cops watching distribution points. And we ain't killers going to a man's house. We soldiers. We take what he values most—his cash flow."

"What about the Colombian shit?" Dre asked, always thinking two moves ahead. "If Bishop really got cartel money behind him, we ain't just hitting a local dealer—we're poking a bear that could swallow us whole."

"Then the cartel gonna be real interested in why their investment can't protect his own stash house." D Roc's smile was cold. "We hit him hard enough, maybe they decide he ain't worth backing no more. Let them eat their own."

"That's a lot of 'maybes' for a one-way trip," Dre said, shaking his head. "What's our exit strategy if this goes sideways?"

"Same as always. Move fast, shoot straight, don't get caught."

"When?" Tone asked.

"Tonight. Two AM. When the city sleeps and the wolves come out." D Roc looked at each of them. "This ain't a game no more. This is war. You ride with me, you might not come back. Any nigga wanna walk away, do it now. No shame."

Nobody moved.

"Good." D Roc pulled out a bottle of Hennessy, took a swig, passed it around. "To Lil Marcus. And to making sure Bishop pays in blood for every tear his mama shed."

They all drank. The bottle made the rounds, communion for the damned.

D Roc went to see Lil Marcus's mama that afternoon. Her apartment was small and sad, photos of Marcus at every age covering the walls like a shrine to a life cut short. She sat on the couch in a bathrobe, eyes empty, a church fan in her lap even though it was cold inside.

"Ms. Johnson," D Roc said quietly, standing in her doorway because he didn't feel worthy of sitting. "I'm sorry. I'm so sorry."

She didn't look at him. "You got my baby killed."

The words hit harder than bullets. D Roc wanted to argue, to explain, to make excuses. But she was right. Marcus was in the game because D Roc made the game look appealing. Made it look like a way out when really it was just a faster way to the cemetery.

"Yes ma'am," he said. "I did."

"You gonna make it right?"

"I'm gonna try."

She finally looked at him, and her eyes were ancient with grief. "Don't try. Do. My boy is gone. But them other boys out there—somebody's sons—they still breathing. You make sure whoever did this don't breathe no more. You hear me?"

"Yes ma'am."

"And then you get out this game." She stood up, walked to him, put a hand on his cheek. "You a good boy underneath all that street. I can see it. Marcus told me you looked out for him. But this life gonna eat you up, baby. It gonna chew you up and spit you out in pieces."

D Roc's eyes burned but he didn't let the tears fall. "I'm already in pieces, Ms. Johnson."

"Then find the glue." She kissed his forehead like she was his own mama. "Before it's too late."

He left her apartment feeling heavier than when he'd arrived. The crown was crushing him now, digging into his skull, drawing blood nobody could see.

Tasha found him at the trap house at six PM, sitting alone in the kitchen, staring at nothing.

"Baby, you gotta eat something," she said, setting down a Styrofoam container of soul food from Sylvia's on Lenox—the kind of place where tourists came for the famous fried chicken but locals came for the memories. Fried chicken, collard greens, mac and cheese—the kind of food that tasted like home even when home was just a memory.

"I ain't hungry."

"You gonna waste away." She sat down across from him. "Talk to me."

"I got a kid killed today."

"You didn't pull the trigger."

"I put the gun in his hand." D Roc finally looked at her, and she could see the cracks forming. "I made him think this life was worth dying for. And now he's gone. Sixteen years old, Tasha. He was supposed to graduate high school next year."

"This ain't on you alone." But her voice was soft, not convincing. "Bishop—"

"Bishop ain't the only villain." D Roc stood up, started pacing. "I'm out here selling poison. I'm out here recruiting kids. I'm out here acting like I'm some kind of king when really I'm just a nigga with a gun and a corner. What kind of kingdom is that?"

"Then stop." She grabbed his hand, made him look at her. "Stop, D. We can leave. Go somewhere new. Start over. You got money saved up—"

"And leave my crew to die? Leave my block to Bishop and them Jersey niggas?" He pulled his hand away. "Nah. I started this. I'm finishing it."

"By getting yourself killed?"

"If that's what it takes."

She slapped him. Hard. The sound echoed in the empty kitchen like a gunshot.

"Don't you dare give up," she hissed, tears streaming down her face. "Don't you dare act like you already dead. I love you. I'm here. I'm real. This—" she grabbed his hand and put it on her chest, over her heart, "—this is real. Don't throw it away for pride."

She was shaking. Crying harder than he'd ever seen her cry. Something felt different about her lately—more raw, more desperate. Like she was holding onto something she couldn't name.

He pulled her close, held her tight, breathed in the smell of her hair. "I love you so much it scares me," he whispered. "But I can't run. I won't. Not from this."

"Then I'm staying too." She pulled back, looked him in the eyes. "If you going to war, I'm going with you."

"Tasha—"

"Don't. I'm not some weak bitch who needs protecting. I grew up in these same streets. I can shoot a gun. I can watch your back. And if you going down, I'm going down with you."

He wanted to argue. Wanted to protect her. But looking in her eyes, he knew she'd made up her mind.

"Okay," he said finally. "Okay."

They held each other in that empty kitchen, two people drowning in a flood of their own making, holding on to each other like life preservers that might not float.

At 1:30 AM, the crew assembled outside Bishop's money house on Lenox. It was a brownstone that looked respectable from the outside—flower boxes in the windows, a painted door, a little fence. Inside was a different story.

D Roc, Tone, Dre, Peezy, and five others approached from different angles. Tasha stayed in the car with Nova and the camera, engine running, ready to be a getaway driver or a witness, whichever came first.

The front door had two guards—big niggas with guns and attitudes. D Roc walked up casual, hands visible, smile on his face.

"Yo, Bishop around?" he asked, friendly as Sunday morning.

"Who's asking?" One of the guards put his hand on his waistband.

"Tell him D Roc came to pay his respects."

The guards looked at each other. One reached for his radio. He didn't get to use it.

Tone came from the left with a tire iron, cracked the first guard across the temple. Dre came from the right, gun to the second guard's head. Both men dropped before they could scream.

"Lights out," D Roc said. "Peezy, tie them up. Everybody else, inside. Quiet and clean."

They moved through the house like ghosts with guns. First floor—empty. Second floor—three counters with money machines, stacks of cash everywhere, and two more guards who went down quick when they saw how many guns were pointed at them.

"Jackpot," Tone whispered, staring at the money. Hundreds of thousands of dollars, maybe more. Bishop's whole operation funding right there.

"Take it all," D Roc ordered. "Every dollar. And burn the rest."

They loaded duffel bags with cash while Dre poured gasoline on the furniture, the walls, the floors. The smell was overwhelming—sharp and chemical and final.

"Anybody else in the house?" D Roc asked one of the tied-up guards.

"Just us, I swear! Please don't burn us alive!"

D Roc looked at the man—young, maybe twenty-five, scared out of his mind. He thought about Lil Marcus. About fire. About choices that led to ashes.

"Drag them outside," he told Tone. "Leave them in the front yard. Let them watch it burn."

They carried the guards out, tied to each other like a chain gang, and left them on the grass. D Roc stood on the front steps, lit a cigarette with a match from the book in his pocket, took one long drag, then tossed the lit match through the open door.

The house went up like it was waiting to burn. Flames climbed the walls, licked the ceiling, reached for the sky like prayers from hell.

D Roc stood there watching, his crew behind him, the heat on his face feeling almost holy.

"That's for Marcus," he said quietly. "And that's for every kid who died for your boss's greed."

Sirens wailed in the distance. Time to go.

They piled into the cars—three of them, full of soldiers and money and smoke that clung to their clothes like guilt. Tasha drove the lead car, hands steady on the wheel, eyes hard.

"You good?" D Roc asked her.

"No," she said honestly. "But I'm here."

That's all either of them could promise anymore. Being here. Being alive. For now.

By dawn, the news was everywhere. Bishop's money house burned to the ground. An estimated three hundred thousand dollars gone. No casualties except Bishop's pride.

D Roc sat in Tasha's apartment, smoking a blunt and watching the news coverage on her little TV. His phone had been ringing nonstop. Congratulations. Threats. Warnings. Everybody had something to say.

Bishop called twice. D Roc didn't answer. Let him stew.

Trey Williams, the Jersey connect, texted one message: *You just made this personal.*

D Roc texted back: *It was always personal.*

Tasha came out the bedroom in one of his t-shirts, nothing else, and curled up next to him on the couch. "What happens now?"

"Now they come for me harder. And I go for them harder." He kissed the top of her head. "Until one side ain't standing no more."

"And which side you think that's gonna be?"

D Roc took a long hit from the blunt, held it, let it out slow. "Honestly? I don't know. But I know I ain't going out quiet."

"King of Nothing," she whispered.

"What?"

"That's what you are. King of Nothing. You got a crown but no kingdom. Got soldiers but no peace. Got money but no future." She looked up at him with sad eyes. "What are you really fighting for, D?"

He didn't have an answer. Or maybe he did and just didn't want to say it out loud.

Pride. Reputation. The only identity he'd ever known.

Outside, the sun was rising over a city that didn't give a fuck about kings or pawns, about battles or truces. The city just kept breathing, kept moving, kept eating its children and calling it survival.

D Roc closed his eyes and wondered if Ms. Johnson was right.

Maybe it was time to find the glue.

But not yet.

Not until Bishop and Trey paid in full.

CHAPTER FOUR: EYE FOR AN EYE

The city didn't sleep after the fire.

By 10 AM, every corner from 110th to 145th was buzzing with the news. D Roc had crossed a line, they said. Burning down a money house wasn't just beef—it was blasphemy. In a world where cash was God, he'd just torched a cathedral.

Bishop's response came at noon.

D Roc was at the trap house counting last night's take when Peezy burst through the door, phone in hand, face white as a ghost.

"They got Tone's little sister," Peezy gasped, out of breath like he'd run the whole way. "They snatched her off the street on her way to school."

Everything stopped.

"How old is she?" D Roc asked, already knowing it was bad.

"Thirteen."

The room temperature dropped ten degrees. Tone's sister, Kenya—quiet girl with glasses who was always reading books too big for her age. Smart kid. Good kid. The kind who was supposed to make it out.

"Where's Tone?" D Roc demanded.

"I don't know. He got the call five minutes ago and just ran out. I think he's heading to Bishop's spot on 145th."

"Fuck!" D Roc grabbed his .40, checked the clip. "That's exactly what they want. It's a trap. Dre! Get everybody! We going to 145th now!"

They piled into two cars—D Roc's Charger and Dre's beat-up Tahoe with tinted windows and a hole in the floor. Seven deep, all strapped, all knowing this might be a one-way trip.

Tasha called as they pulled off. D Roc put her on speaker.

"I heard," she said, voice tight. "Baby, be careful. This feels wrong."

"It is wrong. They got a kid."

"I know. That's why it's a trap. They know you'll come. They know Tone will lose his mind." She paused. "I'm scared."

"Me too." He said it honest because at this point, what was the use in lying? "But I can't let them hurt that little girl. I can't."

"I know. That's why I love you." Her voice cracked. "Come back to me."

"I will."

He hung up knowing it might be the last time they spoke.

The spot on 145th was a commercial building that used to be a bodega before Bishop bought it and turned it into a distribution center. Heavy metal shutters, cameras on every corner, guards posted outside with the kind of body armor that said "shoot me and find out nothing happens."

Tone was already there, pacing like a caged animal, gun in hand, tears streaming down his face.

"They got my baby sister!" he screamed when he saw D Roc. "These motherfuckers got Kenya! I'm gonna kill all of them! I'm gonna—"

D Roc grabbed him by the shoulders. "Listen to me. You go in there hot, they kill you and her both. We do this smart."

"Smart? SMART?" Tone shoved him. "They got my little sister, Roc! My mama's baby girl! What's smart about that?"

"What's smart is getting her out alive." D Roc's voice was steel. "We go in guns blazing, she's the first one they shoot. We play it cool, we might have a chance."

Before Tone could respond, the metal shutter rolled up. Bishop stood in the doorway, flanked by Jersey boys with MAC-10s and bad attitudes. Behind them, visible through the doorway, was Kenya—tied to a chair, tape over her mouth, eyes wide with terror but no visible injuries. Yet.

"D Roc!" Bishop called out, arms spread like he was hosting a party. "Glad you could make it. And Tone—my man—we need to talk about your sister's tuition."

"Let her go," Tone growled, taking a step forward. Three red laser sights appeared on his chest.

"Easy, tiger." Bishop smiled. "Here's the deal. That was three hundred grand you burned last night. I want it back. Plus interest. Plus damages. Call it half a million. You get me that by midnight, Kenya goes home. You don't—" he shrugged, "—well, accidents happen."

"You know we don't got that kind of money," D Roc said.

"Then you better start robbing banks." Bishop checked his watch like he had somewhere to be. "Clock's ticking. Oh, and D? Come alone with the money. Just you. Any of your boys try to follow, any cops show up, any heroic bullshit—the girl dies. Simple as that."

"How do I know you'll let her go?"

"You don't. But what choice you got?" Bishop laughed—a cruel, hollow sound. "Welcome to chess, baby boy. Your move."

The shutter rolled back down.

Tone tried to run at it. Dre and Peezy had to physically drag him back to the car, kicking and screaming like his heart was being ripped out. Maybe it was.

Back at the trap house, they did the math. Between what they had stashed and what they could move in the next twelve hours, they might—MIGHT—get to three hundred thousand. Half a million was impossible.

"So what do we do?" Peezy asked, looking at D Roc like he had answers. He didn't.

"We get creative." D Roc pulled out his phone, scrolled through contacts, found the one he was looking for. "Everybody out. I need to make a call."

Once they were alone, he dialed. It rang four times before a voice answered—smooth, professional, dangerous.

"Rodrigo speaking."

"It's D Roc. I need a favor."

Rodrigo Mendez was a Dominican kingpin who controlled most of Washington Heights. They'd done business before—respectful, professional, no beef. D Roc moved some of his product, Rodrigo took a cut, everybody ate.

"What kind of favor?" Rodrigo asked, suspicious already.

"The expensive kind. I need a loan. Half a million. Today."

Silence. Then laughter. "You're joking."

"Do I sound like I'm joking?"

"D, my friend, I like you. You're smart, you don't cause problems in my territory, you pay on time. But half a million? That's not a loan. That's a mortgage on your life."

"They got a kid. Thirteen-year-old girl. My boy's little sister. I don't pay, they kill her."

More silence. Rodrigo had kids too. Three daughters. That meant something in this world of monsters.

"What's the terms?" Rodrigo asked finally.

"I pay you back a million. Double. Six months."

"And if you can't?"

"Then you own my territory. All of it. 118th, the trap houses, the corners, the crew. Everything."

Rodrigo whistled low. "That's steep. You really gonna risk your whole empire for one kid?"

"She's thirteen, Rodrigo. She reads books and wants to be a doctor. She ain't in the game. She's innocent."

Rodrigo glanced at the photos on his desk. His eight-year-old. His twelve-year-old. His fifteen-year-old who wanted to be a lawyer.

"Innocent don't mean much in our world."

"It should."

"Yeah." Rodrigo's voice went quiet. "It should."

Another pause. D Roc could hear voices in the background, Rodrigo talking to someone in Spanish too fast to follow.

"Okay," Rodrigo said. "I'll do it. But D? You miss one payment, I'm not sending collectors. I'm sending undertakers. Understood?"

"Understood."

"Meet me at the Heights in two hours. Bring the girl's brother. I want to see if this is real or just you playing hero."

"It's real."

"Good. Because if you're lying to me, we're gonna have problems that even you can't shoot your way out of."

The line went dead.

D Roc sat there for a minute, staring at his phone, realizing he'd just gambled everything he'd built on a thirteen-year-old girl he'd only met twice.

But what else could he do? Let her die? That wasn't living anyway.

Washington Heights at 3 PM was like stepping into a different country. Spanish music poured from cars, dominos clacked on card tables, the smell of pernil and rice made his stomach growl despite everything.

Rodrigo's spot was a restaurant called El Paraiso—The Paradise. Ironic name for a place run by the devil.

They met in the back room. Rodrigo was late forties, silver at his temples, expensive suit, rings that cost more than cars. He looked like a banker, not a killer. That made him more dangerous.

The office walls told a story. Photos everywhere—three girls at different ages, quinceañera portraits, graduation caps, a family vacation somewhere tropical. On the desk, a framed picture of a woman with Rodrigo's eyes and a smile that said she'd never seen what her husband really did for a living.

"D Roc." They shook hands. "And this must be Tone."

Tone looked like death warmed over. Red eyes, shaking hands, jaw clenched so tight it might crack.

Rodrigo caught D Roc looking at the photos. "My daughters," he said. "Fifteen, twelve, and eight. The oldest wants to be a lawyer. Can you imagine?

A lawyer." He laughed softly. "She doesn't know what her father does. None of them do. And I plan to keep it that way."

He gestured for them to sit. They did. A man brought coffee. Nobody drank it.

"Tell me about your sister," Rodrigo said to Tone, and something shifted in his eyes. Softer. Like he was thinking about his own girls.

"Her name is Kenya," Tone said, voice barely above a whisper. "She's thirteen. Straight-A student. Wants to go to medical school. She's never done nothing wrong her whole life. She don't even know what I do for real. Thinks I work construction."

"And they took her to get to you?"

"To get to me," D Roc corrected. "I burned Bishop's money house last night. This is retaliation."

Rodrigo nodded slowly. "I heard about that. Bold move. Stupid, but bold." He leaned back in his chair. "You understand what you're asking me? Half a million dollars is not small money. I don't hand that out for sob stories."

"I understand."

"And you understand what happens if you can't pay me back?"

"I understand."

"Good." Rodrigo snapped his fingers. One of his men brought over a duffel bag, set it on the table. "Count it if you want."

"I trust you."

"Smart man." Rodrigo smiled, but it didn't reach his eyes. "You got six months. Million dollars. Miss a payment, I take your territory piece by piece. Miss two payments, I take your life. Miss three—" he looked at Tone, "—I take everyone you love. Crystal clear?"

"Crystal."

"Then we have a deal." Rodrigo stood, extended his hand again. D Roc shook it, feeling like he'd just signed a contract with the devil in blood.

They left El Paraiso with the duffel bag feeling heavier than it should. Five hundred thousand dollars in cash. Kenya's ransom. D Roc's entire future riding on what happened next twelve hours.

"Thank you," Tone said in the car, tears falling again. "Thank you, Roc. I can't—I don't—"

"Save it. Just get your sister back. That's all the thanks I need."

At 11:45 PM, D Roc stood outside the 145th Street spot. Alone. Duffel bag in hand. Gun on his hip but knowing he probably wouldn't get a chance to use it.

Across the street, hidden in shadows, Dre and Peezy watched through scopes. Nova was in a building two blocks over with a long lens and a direct line to D Roc's ear via a wireless earpiece Rodrigo had provided. If this went bad, at least there'd be witnesses.

At 11:58, the shutter rolled up. Bishop stood there again, but this time Trey Williams was with him—tall, light-skinned, cold eyes that had probably seen more bodies than a morgue.

"You came," Bishop said, sounding genuinely surprised. "And alone. I'm impressed."

"I got your money. Where's the girl?"

"Show me the money first."

D Roc tossed the duffel bag at Bishop's feet. One of the Jersey boys opened it, checked the stacks, nodded confirmation.

"It's all there," Bishop said. "I counted twice. See, D? This is how business should be conducted. No shooting, no burning. Just money and respect."

"Kenya. Now."

Bishop gestured behind him. Another Jersey boy brought Kenya out. She was crying, shaking, but alive. Her eyes locked on D Roc like he was salvation.

"Let her go," D Roc said.

"Of course." Bishop cut her zip-ties himself. "Run along, sweetheart. Sorry for the misunderstanding."

Kenya ran. Straight to D Roc, collapsed against him, sobbing. He held her with one arm, his other hand still near his gun.

"We're even now," Bishop said. "You burned my house, I took your money. Eye for an eye. No hard feelings."

"This ain't over," D Roc said quietly.

"No?" Trey Williams spoke for the first time. His voice was like gravel and smoke. "Maybe it should be. You lost money tonight. We lost money last night. We could keep bleeding each other, or we could—"

A shot rang out.

Then another.

Then everything went to hell.

The shots came from the building behind Bishop—not from D Roc's crew, but from somewhere else. A Jersey boy dropped, skull opened like a melon. Another caught one in the throat.

"Ambush!" Bishop screamed, diving back inside.

But it wasn't D Roc's ambush.

More shots, from different angles, tearing apart the street like swiss cheese. Car alarms wailing. Glass shattering. Screams echoing off buildings.

D Roc grabbed Kenya and ran, half-carrying her back toward where Dre and Peezy were stationed. Bullets chased them, kicking up concrete, pinging off metal.

"Who the fuck is shooting?" Peezy's voice in his ear.

"Not us!" D Roc dove behind a car, Kenya underneath him, his body her shield. "Somebody's hitting both sides!"

Through the chaos, D Roc saw Trey Williams get clipped in the shoulder, saw Bishop's guards return fire blindly at buildings they couldn't see into. Saw Dre and Peezy doing the same, confused, outgunned.

Then, just as suddenly as it started, the shooting stopped.

Sirens in the distance. Lots of them.

"Fall back!" D Roc ordered. "Everybody out! Now!"

They scattered like roaches. D Roc carried Kenya to the Charger, threw her in the backseat, and burned rubber getting out of there. In his rearview, he saw Bishop's crew doing the same, saw bodies on the ground—at least five, maybe more.

"What the fuck was that?" Kenya sobbed, hunched down in the backseat.

"I don't know, baby girl. But you're safe now. I'm taking you to your brother."

He met up with Tone at a safe house on 132nd. The reunion was beautiful and heartbreaking—Tone holding his sister, both of them crying, thanking God and D Roc in equal measure.

But D Roc wasn't celebrating.

Somebody had just tried to kill both him and Bishop at the same time. Somebody with resources and balls big enough to ambush two crews at once.

His phone buzzed. Unknown number.

Unknown: *You're welcome. Consider this a warning. Leave or join us. Those are your only options. - The Colombians*

D Roc stared at the message, his blood running cold.

The Colombians. The real players. The suppliers who made Bishop and Rodrigo look like corner boys. They'd been quiet for years, letting the locals fight over scraps.

But apparently, they were done being quiet.

And D Roc had just found himself in the middle of a war he didn't even know existed.

He texted back: *Who the fuck is this?*

Unknown: *Your future boss or your executioner. Depends on your answer. We'll be in touch.*

D Roc closed his eyes and leaned against the wall.

First Bishop. Then Trey. Then Rodrigo's loan. Now the Colombians.

He was drowning. Not in water but in blood and debt and bodies. Every breath felt like he was inhaling the ashes of everything he'd burned.

CHAPTER FIVE: THE DEVIL YOU DON'T KNOW

The next morning, D Roc woke up to his phone vibrating off Tasha's nightstand like it was having a seizure.

Fifteen missed calls. Twenty-three texts. The streets were on fire with rumors about last night's ambush. Some said it was the feds finally making their move. Others swore it was a rival crew from the Bronx. Nobody was saying Colombians because nobody wanted to believe the Colombians gave a fuck about Harlem.

But D Roc knew better.

He rolled out of bed, careful not to wake Tasha who was curled up like she was trying to disappear into the sheets. The apartment was cold despite the summer heat outside. Or maybe that was just him. Maybe he'd been cold for a while now and just stopped noticing.

His phone rang again. Rodrigo.

"Yeah," D Roc answered, voice rough from too many cigarettes and not enough sleep.

"We need to talk. Now." Rodrigo didn't wait for a response. "El Paraiso. One hour. Come alone."

The line went dead.

D Roc stared at his phone, wondering if this was about the money he already owed or about the new problem neither of them had seen coming. Either way, it wasn't good.

He found a Newport, sparked it on the stove, and smoked it while staring out the kitchen window at a city that looked peaceful from five stories up. From up here, you couldn't see the blood on the concrete or the needles in the gutters. From up here, Harlem almost looked beautiful.

Almost.

El Paraiso was quieter during the day. No music, no dominos, just the smell of coffee and the sound of dishes being washed in the back. Rodrigo sat at the same table as last time, but now there was someone with him—a woman in her fifties, elegant, expensive jewelry, eyes that had seen empires rise and fall.

"D Roc," Rodrigo said without getting up. "Meet Carmen Vasquez. She's—"

"I know who she is," D Roc said, suddenly very aware of the .40 on his hip and how useless it would be if things went sideways.

Carmen Vasquez. The name alone made soldiers shake. She wasn't flashy like the male kingpins. She didn't need to be. She moved cocaine through the entire East Coast like it was legal commerce. Whispers said she had judges, senators, and police chiefs on her payroll. Whispers also said she'd once had a man skinned alive for stealing twenty kilos.

D Roc didn't know if that last part was true, but looking at her calm face, he believed it.

"Sit," Carmen said. It wasn't a request.

He sat.

Carmen studied him for a long moment before speaking. There was something in her eyes that D Roc hadn't expected—not warmth exactly, but recognition. Like she was looking at a younger version of something she remembered.

"I was sixteen when I killed my first man," she said quietly. "He worked for a rival who thought my family was weak because my father had just died. I proved him wrong." She paused, let the words settle. "I tell you this so you understand—I know what you are because I was you once. The difference is I got smart before the streets ate me alive."

"You've become quite famous in just a few days," Carmen continued, her English perfect but carrying the weight of an accent that said she'd learned it as a second language and still thought in Spanish. "Burning money houses. Kidnapped children. Midnight shootouts. Very dramatic."

"I didn't start it."

"But you've certainly escalated it." She sipped her coffee like they were discussing the weather. "Do you know why I'm here, Mr. Roc?"

"To tell me I'm in your way."

She smiled. It was worse than if she'd frowned. "Rodrigo tells me you're smart. He's right. Yes, you're in my way. But more importantly, you're making noise. And noise attracts attention. Federal attention. The kind that costs me millions in lost shipments and lawyers."

"So what do you want?"

"I want silence." She set down her cup with a delicate clink. "I want Bishop gone. I want these Jersey boys—Trey and his idiots—gone. I want the streets calm so my business can flow like water, quiet and profitable."

"And if I can't do that?"

"Then I'll do it myself. But I promise you, my methods are far less discriminating. I don't care about innocence or guilt. I don't care about children or grandmothers or priests. I care about profit. So when I clean house, I burn the whole structure down, foundation included."

The threat was clear. She'd kill everyone—his crew, Tasha, innocent bystanders—anyone connected to the noise.

"What exactly are you asking me to do?"

Carmen leaned forward. "Bishop is protected by my organization because he moves product. But he's become sloppy, emotional, stupid. I'm giving you permission—no, I'm ordering you—to remove him. Permanently."

"You want me to kill Bishop."

"I want the problem solved. How you solve it is your business." She pulled out an envelope, slid it across the table. "There's fifty thousand dollars in there. Consider it a down payment for services rendered. When Bishop is gone, there'll be another hundred. And when Trey and his Jersey boys are gone, another two hundred."

D Roc stared at the envelope like it was a snake. "And if I say no?"

"Then you're part of the problem." Carmen stood, smoothed her dress. "And I solve problems. All of them. You have one week, Mr. Roc. Seven days. After that, my people handle it, and trust me, you don't want to be anywhere near Harlem when that happens."

She left, heels clicking on the tile floor like a countdown.

Rodrigo waited until she was gone before speaking. "Take the money, D."

"She's asking me to be a hitman."

"She's giving you a way out." Rodrigo lit a cigar, the smoke thick and sweet. "You owe me a million dollars. You think you can make that hustling corners? You'll be lucky to clear fifty grand in six months. But this?" He tapped the envelope. "This is three-fifty for two bodies. Bodies that were probably gonna end up dead anyway. And it clears your debt with me, plus leaves you with cash to spare."

"And makes me a hired killer for the Colombians."

"You're already a killer, D. Don't pretend this is about morality." Rodrigo's voice went hard. "This is about survival. Carmen doesn't make offers twice. You walk out of here without that envelope, you're signing your own death warrant. And Tasha's. And everyone you care about."

D Roc's hand hovered over the envelope. Inside was blood money. Outside was a war he couldn't win. Between a rock and a hard place, they say. But this felt more like being between a bullet and a grave.

He took the envelope.

"Smart man," Rodrigo said, smiling again. "One week. Make it clean."

D Roc sat in the Charger for twenty minutes, engine off, staring at the envelope in his lap. Fifty thousand dollars to become an executioner. Three hundred fifty total to murder two men.

His phone rang. Tasha.

"Where are you?" She sounded worried. She was always worried now.

"Handling business."

"What kind of business?"

"The kind I can't talk about on the phone." He started the engine. "I'll be home soon."

"D—"

"I love you," he said, and meant it more than he'd ever meant anything. "Remember that."

"You're scaring me."

"I'm scared too."

He hung up before she could respond, before he could hear the fear in her voice turn to panic. He pulled into traffic, heading back to Harlem, back to the trap house, back to the only life he'd ever known.

The envelope sat on the passenger seat like a passenger he didn't want.

The crew was at the trap house when he arrived—Tone, Dre, Peezy, Nova with his ever-present camera, and a few others who'd proven loyal. They were cleaning guns, counting product, doing the daily work of survival.

"We got problems," D Roc announced, dropping the envelope on the table. "Big ones."

He told them everything. The Colombians. Carmen Vasquez. The contract on Bishop and Trey. The one-week deadline. The fifty grand sitting right there in front of them.

The room went quiet.

"You're gonna do it?" Tone asked finally. "You're gonna kill Bishop? My mama always said once you kill for money, you ain't nothing but a hired gun. That who we are now?"

"Do I got a choice?" D Roc pulled out a Newport, sparked it. "Carmen made it real clear—either I handle it, or she handles all of us."

"Hold up—what's the exit strategy here?" Dre leaned forward, always thinking three moves ahead. "We do this hit, then what? We just keep killing for her? What's the endgame?"

"We're survivors," D Roc said. "And survivors do what they gotta do."

Peezy picked up the envelope, peeked inside, whistled low. "Yo! That's more paper than I seen in my whole life! We really getting fifty bands just to—"

"Blood money," Nova cut him off quietly. The kid had been silent until now, just watching, filming. "That's what that is. Every dollar in there got somebody's death attached to it. You take it, you're not a hustler no more. You're a character in someone else's story. The villain."

"I been a killer," D Roc said, voice flat. "We all have. We just didn't get paid this good for it."

"That's different." Nova stood up. "We killed to protect our block. To protect each other. This? This is murder for money. That's a line, D. Once you cross it, you can't come back. Trust me—I've seen how these stories end."

"Maybe I don't wanna come back." D Roc crushed his cigarette in the ashtray, harder than he needed to. "Maybe I'm tired of pretending I'm something I'm not. I'm a drug dealer. I'm a gangster. I'm the nigga your mama warned you about. Why should I care about lines?"

"Because Tasha does," Nova said simply. "Because that woman loves you, and when she finds out you did this, it's gonna break her heart."

The truth of it hit like a fist. D Roc wanted to argue, to defend himself, to explain that he didn't have a choice. But Nova was right. Tasha would see this as the moment he stopped being her man and started being just another monster in the streets.

"I don't got a choice," D Roc repeated, but it sounded weaker now.

"We always got choices," Nova said. "Sometimes they're all bad. But we still gotta choose. That's what separates the heroes from the villains in any story—not what happens to them, but what they choose when everything's falling apart."

"Then I choose to live." D Roc grabbed the envelope, stuffed it in his jacket. "Bishop dies. Trey dies. We get paid, we clear our debt with Rodrigo, and we live to fight another day. That's the choice."

"And what about after?" Tone shook his head slowly. "You really think Carmen just gonna let us be once we do her dirty work? My sister Kenya—she's thirteen, D. What kind of world am I building for her? We'll be on

Carmen's payroll forever. Every time she got a problem, she'll call us. We'll never be free."

"We already ain't free," D Roc said. "We trapped by the game, by the streets, by the life. At least this way we get paid for our cage."

That night, D Roc and Tasha sat on her couch, passing a blunt back and forth, not talking, just existing in the same space. She'd cooked dinner—rice and beans and chicken, the kind of food that tasted like home even when home was a memory.

"You gonna tell me what's wrong?" she asked after the blunt was finished.

"Everything."

"Be specific."

He laughed, but it was bitter. "I got a week to kill two people or everybody I love dies. How's that for specific?"

She sat up, faced him. "What are you talking about?"

He told her. All of it. The Colombians, Carmen, the contract, the money. He didn't sugarcoat it or dress it up. He laid it out raw and bloody, the way it was.

When he finished, Tasha was crying.

"You can't," she whispered. "Baby, you can't do this. This is different. This is—"

"I have to."

"No, you don't." She grabbed his face, made him look at her. "We can run. Tonight. We can take what money we got and go. Leave the city. Leave the game. Start over somewhere they'll never find us."

"They'll find us. Carmen got reach everywhere. And even if we ran, what about Tone? Dre? Peezy? All the people who depend on me? I leave, they die."

"So stay and become a monster to save them?" She was angry now, tears turning to fire. "That's the choice? Be a hitman or watch everyone die?"

"Yeah. That's the choice."

"Then it's not a choice at all. It's a trap." She pulled away from him, hugged herself. "And the worst part is, you're gonna do it. I can see it in your eyes. You already decided."

"Tasha—"

"Don't." She held up a hand. "Don't explain it away. Don't make it sound reasonable. You're gonna kill two men for money. That's what this is. And when you do, you're gonna be different. You're gonna be the kind of man I can't love anymore."

"Don't say that."

"Why not? It's true." She wiped her eyes. "I fell in love with a hustler, not an executioner. I fell in love with a man trying to survive, not a killer for hire. And once you cross this line, you ain't coming back. We ain't coming back."

He wanted to argue. Wanted to promise her it would be okay. But he'd already broken too many promises to make another one he couldn't keep.

"I'm sorry," was all he could say.

"Me too."

She went to the bedroom and closed the door. D Roc sat on the couch alone, staring at the fifty thousand dollars sitting on the coffee table, wondering when exactly he'd stopped being human and started being just another weapon in someone else's war.

His phone buzzed. Unknown number. Carmen.

Carmen: *Six days left. The clock is ticking.*

D Roc looked at the message, looked at the closed bedroom door, looked at the money that was supposed to save him but was really just a down payment on his soul.

He was starting to understand what that really meant.

CHAPTER SIX: THE LINE

Three days passed like a slow death.

D Roc spent them watching Bishop—learning his patterns, his routines, the moments when he was vulnerable. Bishop was a creature of habit, and habits got men killed.

Every morning at 10 AM, Bishop left his brownstone on 138th Street and walked two blocks to a barbershop on Malcolm X Boulevard. Same barber, same chair, same ninety-minute ritual. He'd get a cut, a shave, a shoe shine. He'd hold court like a mayor, talking loud about nothing important, making sure everyone saw him, respected him, feared him.

That's where D Roc would take him.

Nova set up cameras. Dre mapped the exits. Tone timed the traffic patterns. Peezy bribed the barber's assistant—a young Dominican kid who needed money more than he needed loyalty—to make sure Bishop's regular appointment stayed regular.

It was Friday. Day six of Carmen's deadline. Tomorrow would be too late.

D Roc sat in the Charger across the street from the barbershop, smoking his tenth Newport of the morning, watching the door. Tone was in the passenger seat cleaning a Glock 19 with the kind of focus that came from knowing you might have to use it.

"You sure about this?" Tone asked, not for the first time.

"No."

"Good. Man who's sure about murder ain't got a soul."

"I lost mine a while ago." D Roc crushed the cigarette in the ashtray. "Let's just get it done."

At 9:47 AM, Bishop's black Escalade pulled up. He climbed out wearing a cream suit that probably cost more than most people's rent, gold chain catching the morning light like a target. Two bodyguards flanked him—big niggas with the kind of builds that came from prison yards and protein shakes.

They walked into the barbershop together. Through the window, D Roc could see Bishop settling into his chair, the barber draping him with the cape, the bodyguards taking positions near the door and the back exit.

"Dre, you in position?" D Roc spoke into the burner phone on speaker.

"Yeah. Back alley. Got the exit covered."

"Peezy?"

"Roof across the street. I got eyes on everything."

"Nova?"

"Filming. And praying. Not sure which one matters more."

D Roc checked his .40 one more time. Full clip. One in the chamber. Safety off. He looked at Tone. "You don't gotta do this. This is my job. Carmen's paying me."

"Kenya's safe because of you." Tone's voice was steel. "I ride with you. Always."

They got out of the car and crossed the street like they belonged there. The morning was hot already, humidity making the air thick enough to choke on. A woman pushing a stroller smiled at them. An old man sweeping his stoop nodded good morning. They had no idea they were watching dead men walking.

The barbershop door jingled when they entered.

Everything happened fast and slow at the same time.

Bishop's bodyguards reached for their guns. D Roc shot the first one twice—chest and head. The man dropped like a puppet with cut strings. Tone got the second one—three shots, center mass, the bodyguard's gun clattering to the floor unfired.

Customers screamed. The barber ran. Bishop sat in his chair, frozen, hands up, cape still around his neck like he was waiting for a different kind of cut.

"D Roc," Bishop said, and for the first time since they'd met, there was real fear in his voice. "We can talk about this. We can—"

"You kidnapped a thirteen-year-old girl."

"Business! It was just business!"

"So is this." D Roc raised the .40, barrel pointed at Bishop's face.

"Wait! Wait! I got money! I got connections! I can make you rich! I can—"

"You can shut the fuck up." D Roc's hand was steady. Steadier than his heart. "You wanted a war. You got one. And in war, soldiers die."

"I'm not a soldier, I'm a—"

The shot was loud in the small space. Bishop's head snapped back. The mirror behind him turned red. His cream suit wasn't cream anymore.

D Roc stood there for a moment, staring at what he'd done. At the body slumped in the barber chair. At the blood pooling on the floor. At the line he'd just crossed that Nova warned him about.

"We gotta go," Tone said, already moving toward the door.

They ran.

Behind them, the barbershop was chaos—screaming, crying, the sound of people calling 911. D Roc and Tone made it to the Charger, tires screeching as they pulled away. In the rearview mirror, D Roc saw the barbershop door, saw people spilling out onto the sidewalk, saw someone pointing at his car.

"Peezy, clear?" he asked into the phone.

"Clear. Nobody saw me."

"Dre?"

"Already gone. Meet at the spot."

"Nova?"

"...I got everything on film." Nova's voice was quiet. "Every second. I don't know if that's evidence or art, but I got it."

"Destroy it. All of it. No evidence."

"You sure? This is—"

"Destroy it. That's an order."

The line went dead.

The safe house on 132nd was actually a run-down apartment that belonged to Dre's aunt who'd died two years ago and nobody bothered to clear out. Peeling wallpaper, furniture covered in sheets, the smell of mothballs and memories.

The crew gathered there like survivors of a shipwreck. Tone, Dre, Peezy, Nova. Everyone breathing hard, coming down from the adrenaline, trying to process what they'd just done.

"We really did it," Peezy said, bouncing on his heels, unable to contain himself. "Yo, we really fucking did it! That's some movie shit right there! Did you see his face when—"

"Don't celebrate," D Roc said, sitting on a sheet-covered couch that puffed dust when he moved. "We just made things worse. Trey's gonna come at us twice as hard now."

"But we got paid, right?" Peezy pulled out his phone, still hyped. "Carmen said a hundred K when Bishop's dead. Bishop's dead. So where's the money? We about to be rich!"

As if on cue, D Roc's phone buzzed. A text from an unknown number with a photo attached—a duffel bag full of cash.

Carmen: *Well done. The first installment is at El Paraiso. Pick it up at your convenience. One down, one to go. Six days for Trey.*

D Roc stared at the message. One hundred thousand dollars for a life. That's what Bishop was worth. That's what D Roc's soul was worth apparently.

"I'll get it," Tone offered.

"No. I did the hit. I'll get the money." D Roc stood up, every muscle aching like he'd been in a fight even though it had lasted less than thirty seconds. "Y'all lay low. Don't post nothing on social media. Don't tell nobody where you were. We was all somewhere else, doing something else, with witnesses that'll swear to it."

"What about the bodies?" Dre asked. "The bodyguards got families. The cops gonna—"

"The cops ain't gonna do shit." D Roc lit a Newport, hands shaking just slightly. "Bishop was a known drug dealer. This'll be filed under gang violence and forgotten in a week. That's how it works. We ain't important enough for justice."

"Is that supposed to make me feel better?" Nova asked. The kid looked sick, like he might throw up. "We just killed three people, D."

"You didn't kill nobody. You filmed. That's different."

"Is it? I was there. I helped plan it. I'm an accessory. In the eyes of God, I'm just as guilty."

"Then we'll all burn together." D Roc headed for the door. "I'll be back in an hour. Don't leave. Don't answer the door. Don't do shit."

El Paraiso was closed when he arrived, but the door was unlocked. Inside, Rodrigo sat at a table with the duffel bag between his feet and a cigar between his fingers.

"The prodigal killer returns," Rodrigo said, smiling. "Carmen called. Said you handled it clean. Professional."

"Professional," D Roc repeated, like the word tasted bad. "That what we calling it?"

"That's what I call it when a job gets done right." Rodrigo pushed the bag across the floor with his foot. "One hundred grand. Count it if you want, but it's all there."

D Roc picked up the bag. It was heavy. Blood money always was.

"How do you do it?" he asked. "How do you kill people and sleep at night?"

Rodrigo took a long pull from his cigar, blew smoke toward the ceiling. "I remind myself they would've killed me first if they had the chance. In this life, it's eat or be eaten. You chose to eat. Don't apologize for having teeth."

"But don't you ever—" D Roc struggled with the words. "Don't you ever feel like you're losing yourself? Like every body makes you less human?"

"No." Rodrigo's face was serious now. "Because I never pretended to be human to begin with. This world, this life—it don't reward humanity. It rewards strength. And sometimes strength looks like violence. You can cry about it, or you can cash the check and move on."

"That's fucked up."

"That's survival." Rodrigo stood, buttoned his jacket. "Now get out of here. You got six days to find Trey Williams and finish this. And D? Next time, don't bring your conscience to a murder. It'll get you killed."

D Roc went to Tasha's apartment even though he knew she wouldn't want to see him. He let himself in with his key. She was on the couch watching the news—coverage of the barbershop shooting. Three dead, including notorious drug dealer Marcus "Bishop" Hayes. The reporter was saying it looked like a professional hit.

She had her hand on her stomach. Not holding it exactly, just resting there. Something about the gesture looked different. Protective. Like she was guarding something.

Tasha didn't look at him when he entered.

"I saw," she said quietly. "It's all over the news."

"Tasha—"

"Don't." She stood up, still not looking at him. "Don't try to explain it. Don't make excuses. You killed three people today. Three. And for what? Money?"

"For survival. Carmen would've—"

"I don't care what Carmen would've done!" She finally turned to face him, and her eyes were red from crying. "You had a choice. You always have a choice. And you chose murder. You chose money over morality. You chose to be exactly what everyone says you are—a killer."

"I did it for us. The money clears my debt with Rodrigo. It keeps us safe—"

"Safe?" She laughed, but it was bitter and broken. "Baby, we ain't safe. We never gonna be safe. You're a hitman for the cartel now. They own you. Every time Carmen snaps her fingers, you gonna jump. Every time she points at someone, you gonna shoot. That's not safety. That's slavery."

He wanted to argue. Wanted to tell her she was wrong. But she wasn't.

"I love you," he said instead, because what else was there?

"I love you too," she whispered. "But love ain't enough no more. Love can't wash off blood. Love can't bring back the dead. Love can't save you from what you're becoming."

"What am I becoming?"

"A monster." She walked to the bedroom, paused at the door. "I need you to leave. I need time to think. To figure out if I can still be with someone who— " her voice cracked. "Just go, D. Please."

He went.

* * *

Tasha stood at the window after he left and watched him cross 127th to his car. He walked the way he always walked — like the sidewalk owed him rent. Like the streetlights had been hung for him personally. She used to find that beautiful. She used to find it brave.

Tonight it just looked tired. A man rehearsing a swagger nobody was watching anymore.

She closed the blinds. Locked the deadbolt. The chain.

The apartment was so quiet she could hear the clock above the stove. The fridge cycling on. Mrs. Pinckney's TV through the wall — the same Wheel of Fortune Mrs. Pinckney watched every weeknight at seven. Tasha had grown up with that wall. The rhythm of those puzzle solves was the soundtrack of her childhood.

She put her hand on her stomach without meaning to. Caught herself doing it. Took her hand away.

Her phone buzzed on the coffee table. Diane. Her sister had been calling all day — first to ask if she'd seen the news about Bishop, then again, then again. Tasha had let every call go. She let this one go too. Diane lived in Maryland with a husband who fixed cars and two babies and a life Tasha had stopped envying somewhere around her twenty-eighth birthday and started envying again about six months ago.

She thought about calling her mama. Discarded it. Mama would say *I told you about that boy.* Mama had been telling her about that boy since the first time D Roc came to Sunday dinner two years ago in a fitted cap and a chain heavy enough to choke on. *That boy got dead eyes,* Mama had whispered in the kitchen. *That boy already half a ghost.*

Tasha had defended him. Said he was kind to her. Said he was smart and ambitious and trying to do better. Said her mama didn't know him.

Her mama had said, *Baby, I knew him before he was born. I know all of them. Every last one of them got the same eyes when the streets got finished with them. Don't matter what they was before.*

Tasha had stopped going to Sunday dinner.

She walked to the kitchen and started cleaning. That was what she did when she couldn't think. Wiped the counter that didn't need wiping. Reorganized the spice cabinet. Bleached the sink. Her hands moved on their own while her brain ran the math.

Three years with him. She'd watched it happen. Watched the corner pull him further in by inches. She'd told herself each new thing was the last new thing. The first time he came in with a black eye. The first time she saw the gun on his hip in her kitchen. The first time he asked her to drive somewhere and not ask why. The first time he told her *I just need you to be a witness, that's all.*

She'd been the witness in the car on 145th when his crew rolled on Bishop's spot the first time. She'd kept the engine running. She'd told herself that didn't make her a part of it.

It made her a part of it.

The thing she couldn't stop thinking about, scrubbing the sink that was already clean, was that *she had been good once.* Honor roll at Frederick Douglass Academy. Two years at LaGuardia Community College before her mama got sick. A nursing certificate she finished while her mama was in hospice. A job at Harlem Hospital that paid real money. A 401(k). Health insurance. A name they called over the loudspeaker when somebody needed an intake nurse on the third floor.

That woman was still in here somewhere. Tasha could feel her. Asking questions Tasha didn't want to answer.

What are you doing.

Whose life is this.

Why are you waiting in an apartment for a man who killed three people today and used your couch to plan it.

She put the bleach down. Sat on the kitchen floor with her back against the cabinets. Pulled her knees up to her chest the way she used to do when she was a girl and her mama was working the night shift and the apartment scared her.

She did not cry. She had cried already, when D Roc was still in the room, because some part of her had wanted him to see it. The performance was done. He was gone. There was no one to cry for.

She just sat on the floor and felt her own pulse in her throat and counted the beats and waited to know what to do.

She was still sitting there an hour later when the news anchor on the muted TV said the name *Marcus "Bishop" Hayes* again, and the photo behind him showed a man Tasha recognized — not from the news. From a barbecue at her cousin's place in 2019, before any of this started, when D Roc and Bishop had still been on speaking terms and had laughed together over ribs.

Bishop had told her she had a pretty smile.

Bishop had a daughter. Tasha remembered that. Five or six years old, in pigtails, eating a hot dog.

That little girl had a dead father tonight.

Tasha got up off the floor. Turned off the TV. Went to bed in her clothes. Did not sleep.

* * *

D Roc was three blocks away by then.

The sun was setting, painting the sky red and orange like the world was on fire. Maybe it was. Maybe it had been burning for a while and he was just now noticing.

His phone buzzed. Text from Dre.

Dre: *Turn on the news. Trey Williams just put out a statement. You need to see this.*

D Roc pulled up a live stream on his phone. Trey Williams stood in front of cameras, dressed in all black, face hard as stone.

"Bishop Hayes was my brother," Trey said, voice steady but rage simmering underneath. "Not by blood, but by bond. We built empires together. And tonight, he was murdered. Executed in broad daylight like a dog in the street."

Reporters shouted questions. Trey ignored them.

"To whoever did this—you made a mistake. You thought killing Bishop would scare me. But all you did was wake me up. I'm putting a million dollars on the heads of everyone involved. A million. Cash. No questions asked. You want that money? Find the shooters and bring me proof they're dead."

The press conference exploded with noise. Trey walked away from the podium without another word.

D Roc stared at his phone.

A million dollars. On his head. On Tone's. On everyone who was in that barbershop.

He'd killed Bishop and made things infinitely worse.

The crown wasn't just heavy anymore. It was crushing him. Suffocating him. Killing him one breath at a time.

He sat in the Charger and smoked and watched the sun disappear behind buildings that had seen too much blood, too many bodies, too many kings who thought they could win against an unwinnable game.

Tomorrow, he'd have to figure out how to kill Trey Williams before Trey killed him.

Tonight, he'd just sit here and wonder when exactly he'd stopped being Darrell and started being D Roc.

When he'd stopped being human and started being just another weapon.

When he'd crossed the line Nova warned him about and couldn't find his way back.

CHAPTER SEVEN: HUNTED

A million-dollar bounty changed everything.

By Saturday morning, every hustler, corner boy, and wannabe gangster in Harlem was looking for D Roc. Some wanted the money. Some wanted the reputation. All of them wanted him dead.

D Roc couldn't go back to the trap house—too obvious. Couldn't go to Tasha's—she'd made it clear he wasn't welcome, and besides, he wouldn't put that target on her. Couldn't even sleep in his own car without worrying someone would spray it with bullets while he was dozing.

So he moved like a ghost. Different spot every night. Different car every day—borrowed from people who owed him favors and were too scared to say no. He slept in two-hour increments with his .40 on his chest and one eye open.

The crew scattered too. Tone was holed up with his family, protecting Kenya and his mother. Dre went to stay with his girl in the Bronx. Peezy refused to hide and nearly got killed for it—two corner boys tried to jump him outside a bodega on 125th. He put one in the hospital and sent the other running, but the message was clear: nowhere was safe.

By Sunday, D Roc looked like a different man. Unshaven, bags under his eyes dark as bruises, chain gone, gun always within reach. He'd lost weight—hard to eat when every restaurant could be an ambush. He chain-smoked Newports until his lungs hurt and his fingers smelled like tar and regret.

Nova called him on a burner phone. "We need to meet. In person."

"Too dangerous."

"I don't care. This is important."

They met in Marcus Garvey Park at dawn when only the homeless and the hopeless were awake. Nova looked worse than D Roc—eyes wild, hands shaking, camera nowhere in sight.

"I can't do this no more," Nova said without preamble. "I'm out."

"Out?"

"Out of the crew. Out of the game. Out of all of it." Nova pulled out a wad of cash—looked like maybe five grand. "This is everything I saved. I'm giving it to you. Consider it my exit fee or whatever. But I'm done, D. I can't sleep. I can't eat. Every time I close my eyes I see Bishop's face. The blood. The—"

"You didn't pull the trigger."

"I was there!" Nova's voice cracked. "I helped plan it! I filmed the whole thing! In the eyes of God, I'm just as guilty as you. And I can't—I can't live with that. My grandma raised me better. She's probably rolling in her grave knowing what I became."

D Roc wanted to argue, to convince Nova to stay. But looking at the kid's face—young, broken, terrified—he couldn't.

"Where you gonna go?"

"My cousin got a place in Philly. I'm gonna stay there. Get a job. Go back to school maybe. Try to be the person my grandma thought I could be." Nova looked at him with something like pity. "You know what I realized, D? I've been documenting all this with my camera, thinking I was capturing history. But I was really just watching a tragedy unfold frame by frame. Every story like ours ends the same way. Every single one. The details change but the ending don't."

"What ending is that?"

"Alone. Broken. Dead or wishing you was." Nova shook his head. "You should get out too, D. While you still can. This life—it's gonna kill you. If not the bullets, then the guilt. If not the guilt, then the loneliness. You gonna die out here, one way or another."

"I know."

"Then why stay?"

"Because I don't know how to be nothing else." D Roc took the money even though it felt wrong. "Go. Get out. Don't look back. And Nova? Thank you. For everything."

They shook hands. Nova walked away, and D Roc watched him disappear into the morning fog like a ghost ascending. One less soldier. One more person who escaped before the walls closed in.

D Roc was happy for him.

And jealous as hell.

Monday brought rain and blood.

D Roc was in a motel on the edge of Harlem—the kind of place that rented rooms by the hour and didn't ask questions if you paid cash. He was counting what was left of Carmen's money when someone knocked on the door.

Not a polite knock. A cop knock. Hard and insistent and not taking no for an answer.

D Roc grabbed his gun, crept to the door, looked through the peephole. Two men in suits—detectives probably. Shit.

"D Roc! NYPD! Open the door or we're coming in!"

He could run. Window led to a fire escape. He'd done it before. But if they were at the door, they probably had the back covered too. And running just made him look guilty. Guiltier.

He opened the door, gun behind his back.

"Can I help you, officers?"

The first detective was Black, early fifties, tired eyes that had seen everything twice. His partner was young, white, looked like he still believed in justice. Rookie.

"Detective Morrison," the older cop said, flashing his badge. "This is Detective Chen. We need to talk about Marcus Hayes."

"Who?"

"Bishop. The drug dealer who got his brains blown out in a barbershop Friday morning." Morrison pushed past him into the room, uninvited. "You know anything about that?"

"Should I?"

"Word on the street says you and Bishop had beef. His money house got burned down. Then he ended up dead. That's quite a coincidence."

"Coincidences happen." D Roc stayed by the door, gun still hidden. "I got an alibi for Friday. I was in the Bronx visiting my girl's family."

"That's funny, because your girl—Tasha Freeman, right?—she says she hasn't seen you in three days." Morrison smiled, but it wasn't friendly. "Seems she's pretty upset with you. Something about you becoming someone she doesn't recognize."

The words hit harder than a fist. Tasha had talked to the cops. She'd told them the truth—that she hadn't seen him, which meant he didn't have an alibi. She hadn't thrown him under the bus exactly, but she hadn't protected him either.

"We had a fight," D Roc said carefully. "Couples fight. Don't mean I killed nobody."

"We'll see." Chen spoke for the first time, voice eager. "We got witnesses putting someone matching your description leaving the barbershop right after the shots. We got shell casings. We got cameras. We're building a case, D Roc. And when we finish building it, we're coming for you."

"Then come." D Roc opened the door wider. "Until then, get the fuck out."

Morrison studied him for a long moment. "You know what I see when I look at you? I see a dead man. Maybe we lock you up, maybe Trey Williams gets you first, maybe you eat your own gun one night when the guilt gets too heavy. But either way, you're already gone. You just don't know it yet."

They left.

D Roc closed the door, locked it, and sat on the bed with his head in his hands. The walls were closing in. The cops were building a case. Trey had put a price on his head. Carmen was counting down the days until her deadline. And Tasha—the only person who'd ever made him feel human—had basically told the police to go ahead and investigate.

He was alone.

Completely, utterly alone.

His phone buzzed. Dre.

Dre: *Peezy's dead. They got him.*

The words didn't make sense at first. D Roc read them three times before they connected.

He called Dre immediately. "What happened?"

"Bounty hunters." Dre's voice was rough, like he'd been crying or screaming or both. "Five of them jumped him outside his mama's building. Broad daylight. They shot him twenty-three times, D. Twenty-three. Didn't just kill him—they executed him. Wanted to make sure there was enough left to collect the bounty."

"Where are you?"

"On my way to his mama's. She's—" Dre's voice broke. "She's losing her mind, Roc. Her baby boy is gone. She keeps asking me why. Why her son? What did he do? And I can't tell her. I can't tell her he died because we killed Bishop. Because we're in a war we can't win."

"I'm sorry."

"Sorry don't bring him back!" Dre was yelling now. "Sorry don't explain to his mama why her nineteen-year-old son got shot like a dog in the street! You started this, Roc! You made the call to burn Bishop's house! You pulled the trigger in that barbershop! And now Peezy's dead because of you!"

The line went dead.

D Roc sat there holding the phone, feeling the weight of it—the weight of Peezy's death, of Lil Marcus before him, of Bishop and his bodyguards, of every body that had piled up since this war started.

King of Nothing.

That's what Tasha called him. And she was right. He had a crown made of corpses and a kingdom built on sand. And now it was all crumbling, taking everyone with it.

He went to Peezy's mama's apartment even though he knew he shouldn't. The building was swarming with cops, yellow tape blocking the entrance where it happened. Blood still stained the concrete—dark, almost black, mixed with rain that hadn't washed it away yet.

D Roc stood across the street, hood up, watching. He saw Dre come out, saw him embrace Peezy's mama—a small woman who looked like she'd aged twenty years in one morning. He saw Tone show up, saw the crew gathering to mourn someone who'd died for a war they didn't start but couldn't escape.

He wanted to go over there. Wanted to pay his respects. But he knew his presence would only make it worse. He was the reason Peezy was dead. His decisions, his choices, his war.

He turned to leave and nearly walked into someone.

A kid, maybe sixteen, wearing a red hoodie and carrying something under his jacket. Their eyes met. Recognition flashed across the kid's face.

"You D Roc," the kid said. Not a question.

"You got the wrong person."

"Nah. I seen your picture. Trey Williams put it up all over. Said a million dollars for proof you dead." The kid pulled out a gun—small, probably a .22, but at this range it didn't matter. His hand was shaking. He was scared. Scared kids with guns were the most dangerous kind.

"You gonna shoot me in broad daylight?" D Roc asked calmly, even though his heart was hammering. "In front of all these cops?"

"Million dollars," the kid repeated, like that explained everything. Maybe it did. "I can get my family out the projects. Get my little sister to a better school. Get my mama off her feet. All I gotta do is—"

"Pull the trigger on a man who never did nothing to you," D Roc finished. "That's what you gotta do. You ready for that? You ready to see my face every time you close your eyes? You ready to be a killer at sixteen?"

The kid's hand shook harder. The gun wavered.

"I was you once," D Roc said softly. "Thought I could hustle my way to something better. Thought the money would fix everything. You know what it fixed? Nothing. It just bought me fancier problems. You pull that trigger, you won't be saving your family. You'll be damning yourself."

"But the money—"

"Ain't worth your soul." D Roc took a step closer. The gun was inches from his chest now. "You wanna shoot me? Go ahead. But know that you'll become me. And trust me, kid—you don't wanna be me."

They stood there, frozen in time, two people at different points on the same doomed road. The kid's finger was on the trigger. D Roc's .40 was still tucked in his waistband, within reach but not drawn. One wrong move and one of them was dying.

The kid lowered the gun.

"Get outta here," he said, voice cracking. "Before I change my mind."

D Roc nodded once and walked away, not running, not looking back. He could feel the kid's eyes on him, could feel how close he'd come to dying on a street corner in the rain.

When he turned the corner, he let out a breath he didn't know he'd been holding.

That night, D Roc called Carmen from a pay phone—one of the few that still worked in Harlem.

"Five days left," Carmen said without preamble. "Where are we on Trey Williams?"

"Working on it."

"Work faster. I don't pay for excuses."

"Your bounty's making it harder. Every person in Harlem is trying to kill me. Can't exactly hunt Trey when I'm being hunted."

"That sounds like a personal problem." Carmen's voice was ice. "You accepted the contract. You killed Bishop. Now finish the job or I'll finish you and hire someone more competent."

"I need help. More men. Better weapons. Something."

A pause. Then: "Fine. Tomorrow night. Pier 47. My people will give you what you need to get this done. But D Roc? This is the last favor. Either Trey dies this week, or you do. Those are your only options."

She hung up.

D Roc stood there in the rain, holding a dead phone, staring at the city that had birthed him and was now trying to bury him.

Somewhere out there, Trey Williams was planning his next move. Somewhere, Tasha was crying over the man she'd loved who'd become a monster. Somewhere, Peezy's mama was planning a funeral for a son who'd died too young in a war that wasn't his.

And D Roc?

D Roc was smoking a Newport in the rain, wondering if the kid with the red hoodie would've been doing him a favor if he'd pulled the trigger.

The crown was so heavy now he could barely stand.

But he had to stand. Had to move. Had to survive five more days

Five more days and one more body.

Then maybe—just maybe—he could rest.

CHAPTER EIGHT: ARSENAL

Pier 47 wasn't the kind of place you went unless you were buying something illegal or dumping something dead.

D Roc arrived at midnight in a stolen Honda—not the same one from before, but close enough to be ironic. The pier stretched out into the Hudson River like a broken finger pointing at New Jersey. Appropriate, since Jersey was where all his problems started.

The air smelled like fish, oil, and bad decisions. Waves lapped against rotted wood pilings. Somewhere in the distance, a foghorn moaned like the city itself was in pain.

Two black SUVs were already there, engines running, headlights off. Professional. Carmen's people didn't fuck around.

D Roc parked fifty feet back, .40 on his lap, every nerve screaming that this was an ambush. But what choice did he have? He needed weapons. He needed help. He needed something to give him an edge against Trey Williams and his thirty-deep Jersey crew.

He got out slow, hands visible, gun tucked in his waistband where they could see he wasn't reaching for it.

A door opened on the lead SUV. A man stepped out—huge, maybe six-five, built like a refrigerator, wearing all black tactical gear. Face like a tombstone. Behind him, three more men, same outfit, same dead eyes.

"You D Roc?" Refrigerator asked. His accent was thick—Colombian, definitely.

"Yeah."

"Carmen says you need tools."

"That's right."

Refrigerator walked to the back of the SUV, opened the trunk. Inside was enough firepower to start a small war. D Roc felt his breath catch.

Two AK-47s with extended mags. Three AR-15s with tactical scopes. A .50 caliber Desert Eagle that looked like it could stop a car. Boxes of ammunition—enough to reload fifty times. Flash grenades. Smoke grenades. Body armor—level III plates that could stop rifle rounds. Night vision goggles. Even a goddamn sniper rifle with a bipod and laser sight.

"Jesus," D Roc whispered.

"Carmen says finish the job." Refrigerator's voice was flat, emotionless. "Trey Williams dies in four days or less. You understand?"

"I understand."

"Good." Refrigerator gestured to his men. They started loading the weapons into D Roc's stolen Honda like they were moving furniture. "One more thing."

He pulled out a phone—expensive smartphone, still in the box.

"Encrypted. Carmen calls you on this, you answer. Always. No matter what." Refrigerator handed it over. "You try to run, we find you. You fail, we kill you. You succeed—" he almost smiled, "—you live long enough to take the next contract."

"What if I don't want another contract?"

"Then you don't understand how this works." Refrigerator closed the trunk of the Honda, now heavy with death. "You work for Carmen now. You accepted her money. You killed for her. You belong to her. Only way out is in a body bag. So do yourself a favor—stay useful."

They left without another word, SUVs disappearing into the night like they'd never been there.

D Roc stood on the pier, smoking a Newport with shaking hands, staring at the car full of military-grade weapons, wondering when exactly he'd stopped being a hustler and started being a professional killer.

The phone Carmen gave him buzzed immediately.

Carmen: *Trey Williams is at a penthouse in Newark. 550 Broad Street. Top floor. Heavy security. Four days. Make it count.*

D Roc stared at the address. Newark. Trey's home turf. Where he had the advantage, the numbers, the loyalty of every corner boy who'd grown up watching him rise.

It was a suicide mission.

But it was the only mission he had.

He drove back to Harlem with enough weapons to overthrow a small country, paranoid every cop car he passed was going to pull him over and find the arsenal. But luck—if you could call it that—was on his side.

He stashed the car in an abandoned garage on 140th Street, covered it with a tarp, padlocked the door. Nobody would find it unless they were looking specifically for it.

Then he walked. Three miles through Harlem at 2 AM, hood up, head down, hand on his .40, jumping at every sound. A cat knocked over a trash can and he almost shot it. A homeless man asked for change and D Roc nearly had a heart attack.

The paranoia was eating him alive.

He ended up at a 24-hour diner on 125th Street, a block down from the Apollo Theater—the kind of place where the coffee tasted like burnt regret and the waitress looked like she'd given up on life in 1987. Through the window, he could see the Apollo's famous marquee glowing in the dark, advertising some show he'd never see. But the diner was public, well-lit, and full of people who were too tired to care about bounties.

D Roc ordered coffee he wouldn't drink and eggs he wouldn't eat and sat in a booth by the window where he could see anyone coming.

His phone—the regular one, not Carmen's—had seventy-three missed calls. Most were unknown numbers, probably people trying to set him up for the bounty. But three were from Tone.

He called back.

"Where the fuck you been?" Tone answered immediately, voice rough. "I been trying to reach you for hours."

"Handling business. What's wrong?"

"Everything's wrong. Dre got jumped tonight. Five niggas ran up on him at a gas station in the Bronx. He shot two of them but caught one in the leg. He's alive but fucked up, bleeding bad. Won't go to the hospital because he knows they'll report the gunshot and the cops'll be on him."

"Where is he?"

"His girl's apartment. But Roc—he's talking crazy. Saying he's done. Saying this ain't worth it. Saying we should've never touched Bishop." Tone's voice dropped. "He's right. We shouldn't have. Look at us—Peezy's dead, Nova's gone, we all got prices on our heads. For what? So you could collect blood money from the Colombians?"

"You blaming me now too?"

"I'm stating facts." Tone didn't sound angry, just tired. Defeated. "We're losing, Roc. We're dying piece by piece. And for what? Territory? Money? Pride? None of it matters if we all dead."

D Roc didn't have an answer. Because Tone was right. They were losing. Not just the war—they were losing themselves. Losing each other. Losing everything that used to matter.

"I got weapons," D Roc said finally. "Serious hardware. Enough to take out Trey and his whole crew."

"And then what? You really think Carmen just lets us walk away after? You really think Rodrigo forgives that million-dollar debt? You really think the cops stop building their case?" Tone laughed, but it was bitter. "We're already dead, Roc. We just don't know it yet."

"So what you saying? We give up? Let Trey kill us? Let Carmen kill us?"

"I'm saying maybe Peezy was the lucky one. He don't gotta live with this shit no more."

The line went dead.

D Roc sat there staring at his phone, feeling the last thread of his crew unraveling. Tone had always been solid. Always loyal. If he was breaking, if he was ready to quit, then everything really was falling apart.

He did the math in his head. The cold arithmetic of loss. Peezy—dead, shot twenty-three times for a bounty. Lil Marcus—dead, burned alive in a stash house. Nova—gone, smart enough to run while he still could. Dre—wounded, bleeding out in the Bronx, done with all of it. Tone—still breathing but breaking, ready to walk away.

Five. He'd started with a crew of twenty. Now he had five, and half of them were ghosts or quitters.

The empire he'd built was down to ashes and memories.

The waitress refilled his coffee without asking. She looked at him with sad eyes that had seen too many young men who wouldn't make it to thirty.

"You okay, baby?" she asked.

"No, ma'am."

"Didn't think so." She set down the pot. "Whatever you running from, it ain't worth your life. Trust me. I seen too many boys like you end up in the ground before they even knew what living was."

"What if I don't know how to stop running?"

"Then you better learn fast. Before the running kills you."

She walked away, leaving D Roc alone with cold coffee and colder truths.

At dawn, he went to check on Dre.

The Bronx apartment was a fourth-floor walkup in a building that should've been condemned ten years ago. D Roc knocked in pattern—three short, two long—their code.

Dre's girl, Shanice, opened the door. She was young, maybe twenty-one, pretty in a tired way. Her eyes were red from crying.

"He's bad," she said without preamble. "Real bad. Won't let me call an ambulance. Won't let me get a doctor. Just keeps saying he's fine when he's obviously not."

Dre was on the couch, leg wrapped in bloody towels, face gray with pain. A bottle of Hennessy sat on the coffee table, half empty. Self-medicating.

"The fuck you doing here?" Dre asked when he saw D Roc. "Came to watch me bleed out?"

"Came to check on you."

"I'm fine." He wasn't. He looked like death was already measuring him for a coffin.

"Let me get you a doctor. Someone who don't report gunshots—"

"I said I'm fine!" Dre tried to sit up, hissed in pain, fell back. "Just go, Roc. You done enough damage."

"Dre—"

"Peezy's dead because of you! We all got targets on our backs because of you! You made a deal with the devil and dragged us all to hell with you!" Dre's voice cracked. "My mama called me yesterday crying. Said people coming around asking about me. Said somebody tried to break into her house. My MAMA, Roc. An old lady who never hurt nobody, and now she's scared because her son's wrapped up in your war."

"I'm sorry."

"Sorry don't fix nothing." Dre grabbed the Hennessy, took a long pull. "I'm out. After this leg heals, I'm gone. Moving to Atlanta. My cousin got a job lined up. Legit job. Construction. Honest money. I'm done with all this."

"You can't run. Trey's got reach—"

"Then I'll die in Atlanta instead of Harlem. At least I'll die trying to be something different." Dre looked at him with eyes that used to respect him but now just looked sad. "You should do the same. While you still can."

D Roc left without another word. On the stairs, Shanice caught up to him.

"He's worse than he's saying," she whispered. "Bullet's still in there. If he doesn't get help soon, infection's gonna kill him. Can you—can you do something? Please?"

D Roc pulled out a stack of bills—five grand from Carmen's money. "Get him to a doctor. Tell them it was a car accident, a work injury, whatever. But get that bullet out."

"Thank you." She hugged him, unexpected and desperate. "And D Roc? Whatever y'all did—whatever this war is about—it ain't worth losing him. Please. Just let it go."

"I wish I could."

By Tuesday afternoon, D Roc was back in Harlem, sitting in the abandoned garage, staring at the weapons Carmen had given him. The AKs. The ARs. The grenades. Enough firepower to take on Trey's crew.

But how?

Trey was in Newark, in a penthouse, surrounded by security. He had thirty soldiers. D Roc had—what? Himself? Tone, maybe, if he could convince him not to quit? Dre was shot and bailing. Nova was gone. Peezy was dead.

He was one man against an army.

The encrypted phone buzzed. Carmen.

"Status?" she asked. No pleasantries. Just business.

"Working on it."

"Work faster. Three days left. I want proof by Friday or I send my people to finish what you started."

"I need more time—"

"You need to make better decisions." Her voice went cold. "Bishop had security too. You still killed him. Figure it out."

She hung up.

D Roc lit a Newport, his hands steady now. Not because he was calm, but because he'd smoked so many cigarettes in the last week that his body had stopped reacting to nicotine. It was just a ritual now. Something to do with his hands that wasn't murder.

His regular phone rang. Unknown number. He almost didn't answer.

"Yeah?"

"D Roc?" A woman's voice, familiar but he couldn't place it.

"Who this?"

"It's Tasha."

His heart stopped. Started again. Stopped.

"Tasha—baby—I—"

"Don't." Her voice was tight, controlled. "I ain't calling to get back together. I'm calling because I heard Dre got shot. Because I heard Peezy's dead. Because I heard you're planning something stupid with Trey."

"How did you—"

"The streets talk. And I still know people." She paused. "D, please. Just stop. Walk away. Leave New York. I'll come with you. We can start over somewhere else. Somewhere they can't find us."

"They'll find us. Carmen's got reach everywhere."

"Then we keep running. Forever if we have to. But at least we'll be alive. At least we'll be together." Her voice broke. "I can't lose you. I know I said I couldn't be with what you became, but I'd rather have the monster you are than the ghost you're gonna be."

D Roc closed his eyes. Pictured it—him and Tasha somewhere far away. Maybe the West Coast. Maybe Mexico. Maybe somewhere where the streets didn't own them and the past couldn't find them.

It was a beautiful dream.

And completely impossible.

"I can't," he whispered. "I owe too much money. Got too many people trying to kill me. Got a contract I gotta finish or everyone I care about dies. I can't run, baby. I gotta see this through."

"Then you're gonna die."

"Probably."

Silence stretched between them, heavy with all the things they couldn't say, all the futures they'd never have.

"You remember that night at Sylvia's?" Tasha asked suddenly, her voice soft. "Our first real date. You wore that terrible gold chain that was too big for you, trying to impress me. And you ordered the fried chicken but you were so nervous you couldn't eat. Just pushed it around your plate while you tried to think of something smooth to say."

D Roc remembered. Remembered being twenty-two and thinking she was the most beautiful woman he'd ever seen. Remembered his hands shaking worse than they did before any gunfight.

"You told me you wanted to take me to Paris someday," Tasha continued. "Said you'd never been anywhere but New York but you'd take me to Paris. And I believed you. I actually believed you."

"I meant it."

"I know you did. That's the worst part." She was crying again. "Somewhere between then and now, you stopped believing it yourself. Stopped believing you could be anything but this."

"I love you," Tasha said finally. "I'm always gonna love you. But I can't watch you die. So this is goodbye."

"Tasha—"

"Be safe, D. And if you somehow survive this, if you somehow make it out—come find me. I'll be waiting."

The line went dead.

D Roc sat there in the garage, surrounded by weapons, smoking a cigarette, crying for the first time since he was a kid.

He cried for Peezy. For Lil Marcus. For his crew falling apart. For Dre bleeding out in the Bronx. For Tone losing faith. For Nova running away. For his mama who'd died when he was twelve and never got to see what he became.

And he cried for Tasha—for the woman who'd loved him when he was human and couldn't love him when he became a monster.

When the tears stopped, all that was left was rage.

Cold, focused, murderous rage.

Three days.

He had three days to kill Trey Williams.

Three days to end this war.

Three days to prove he was still the king of something.

Even if that something was nothing.

He called Tone.

"I need you," D Roc said. "One last time. Then we're done. Win or lose, after this, you walk away clean."

"What are you planning?"

"We're going to Newark. We're taking everything Carmen gave us. And we're killing Trey Williams in his own house."

"That's suicide."

"Yeah. But if we pull it off, we live. We get paid. We clear our debts. We get out."

"And if we don't?"

"Then we die trying instead of waiting around to die hiding."

Tone was quiet for a long time. So long D Roc thought he'd hung up.

"Okay," Tone said finally. "One last job. Then I'm done. I'm taking my mama and Kenya and moving somewhere quiet. Somewhere these streets can't find us."

"Deal."

"When?"

"Tomorrow night. We hit him Thursday. Give me today to plan, tomorrow to execute."

"See you tomorrow then." Tone paused. "And Roc? If we die doing this—at least we die on our feet."

"Like soldiers."

"Like brothers."

The line went dead.

D Roc stood up, crushed his cigarette, and started loading magazines. The AKs. The ARs. The grenades. The body armor. Everything Carmen gave him, everything he needed to start a war.

Tomorrow night, he'd take the war to Newark.

Tomorrow night, he'd either kill Trey Williams or die trying.

Tomorrow night would decide if he was a king.

Or just another body in a city full of them.

But he'd carry it one more day.

One more fight.

One more death.

And then—maybe—he could finally rest.

CHAPTER NINE: NEWARK

Thursday came fast and merciless.

D Roc spent the morning cleaning weapons with the kind of focus that comes from knowing you might die tonight. Each gun got wiped down, oiled, loaded, and tested. The AKs sang their mechanical song. The ARs clicked into place like prayers. The grenades sat in a canvas bag like deadly eggs waiting to hatch.

Tone showed up at noon with body armor under his hoodie and death in his eyes.

"My mama cried this morning," Tone said, sitting on an overturned crate in the garage. "Said she had a bad dream. Said she saw me in a coffin."

"Mamas always know." D Roc handed him an AK, three full magazines taped together for quick reloads. "You still down?"

"Till the end." Tone checked the action, smooth and practiced. "Kenya made me promise to come back. Told her I would."

"Don't make promises you can't keep."

"Little late for that."

They went over the plan one more time. Simple, violent, probably suicidal.

550 Broad Street, Newark. Penthouse apartment, twentieth floor. Trey Williams and however many guards he kept around him. Intel said at least six bodyguards inside, plus building security downstairs.

The play: Hit them at 2 AM when the building was quiet. Bypass security using the service entrance—Tone had bribed a maintenance worker with ten grand. Take the freight elevator to the nineteenth floor. Stairs to twenty. Flash grenades through the door. Storm in with AKs blazing. Kill everyone who moved. Get out before the cops showed up.

Five minutes. In and out. Fast and final.

"We don't make it out," Tone said, "who you want at your funeral?"

"I'm not having one. Throw me in a dumpster and keep it moving."

"Nah, man. You deserve better than that."

"I deserve whatever hell's waiting for me." D Roc loaded the last magazine, slammed it into the AK. "But if I'm going to hell, I'm taking Trey with me."

They left Harlem at 10 PM in a stolen van—panel truck, no windows, perfect for transporting an arsenal. The drive to Newark took forty minutes but felt like hours. Neither of them spoke. Just smoked—D Roc his Newports, Tone his Blacks—and listened to the sound of the engine and their own thoughts.

The city gave way to highway gave way to another city that looked just like the one they left. Same projects, same corners, same broken dreams in different zip codes.

Newark at midnight was alive in the way only hood cities get—restaurants still open, corner boys still hustling, women in heels stumbling out of clubs, bass thumping from car speakers. The city didn't sleep. It just closed its eyes and pretended.

They parked three blocks from 550 Broad Street in an alley behind a Chinese restaurant that had seen better decades. D Roc and Tone put on the body armor—level III plates that added twenty pounds each but might stop a bullet. Might.

They loaded up. AKs with thirty-round mags. .40 on the hip as backup. Flash grenades on the vest. Smoke grenades in pockets. Tactical gloves. Ski masks rolled up on their heads, ready to pull down.

"You scared?" Tone asked.

"Terrified."

"Good. Dead men ain't scared. Long as we scared, we alive."

They moved through the Newark streets like shadows with guns, keeping to alleys and side streets, avoiding cameras and corner boys who'd remember strangers. 550 Broad Street was a luxury building—the kind where drug money went to look legal. Doorman in the front, cameras everywhere, key card access, the works.

But the service entrance in back had a door held open by a brick—maintenance worker had kept his promise. They slipped inside, into a concrete stairwell that smelled like bleach and industrial cleaning solution.

No cameras back here. Just pipes and painted cinderblocks and fluorescent lights that hummed like trapped insects.

The freight elevator was old, slow, and loud. Every floor it climbed sounded like it was screaming for help. D Roc and Tone stood on opposite sides, AKs ready, waiting for the doors to open on guards or cops or death.

Nineteenth floor. Doors opened to empty hallway.

They took the stairs to twenty, slow and careful. Each step calculated. Each breath measured. This was it. The moment everything changed.

At the top of the stairs, D Roc pulled down his ski mask. Tone did the same. They were anonymous now. Just two more killers in a city full of them.

The penthouse door was at the end of the hall—reinforced steel with a peephole and deadbolt. Light came from underneath. Music playing inside, muffled bass.

D Roc held up three fingers. Two. One.

Tone kicked the door just below the knob. It didn't budge. Reinforced frame. D Roc pulled a flash grenade, yanked the pin, and wedged it into the doorframe crack.

"Fire in the hole!"

They dove back as the grenade detonated—a flash of light bright as the sun and a bang that made their ears ring even through the adrenaline. The door blew inward, smoke pouring out.

They went in.

First room was chaos. Two bodyguards stumbling, blind from the flash, reaching for guns they couldn't see to shoot. D Roc's AK spoke first—controlled bursts, center mass, both men dropping before they knew what hit them.

Living room opened to kitchen. Another guard coming around the corner, gun up, eyes wide. Tone's AK rattled—three rounds, the guard's chest erupted red, he fell backward into the refrigerator and slid down, leaving a smear.

"Trey!" D Roc shouted. "We here for you!"

Gunfire answered—automatic, from somewhere deeper in the apartment. Bullets tore through the walls, the couch, the TV. D Roc and Tone dove behind the kitchen counter as the penthouse turned into a warzone.

"How many?" Tone yelled over the gunfire.

"Too many!"

More bodyguards poured out from the bedrooms—at least four, maybe five, all strapped with MAC-10s and ARs, all shooting at once. The kitchen counter shredded under the onslaught. Cabinets exploded. Glass shattered. Plaster dust filled the air like snow.

D Roc popped up, fired a burst, dropped back down. One guard stumbled, hit in the shoulder, kept firing. These weren't amateurs. These were Jersey soldiers who'd been through real wars.

Tone threw a smoke grenade. It hissed and billowed, filling the apartment with thick gray fog. Visibility went to zero.

"Move!" Tone grabbed D Roc and they pushed forward through the smoke, shooting at muzzle flashes, ducking return fire that sounded like fireworks in hell.

A shape loomed in the smoke. D Roc fired point-blank. The shape dropped. Another shape—Tone engaged, short burst, it fell.

Then the smoke started to clear and D Roc saw him.

Trey Williams. Standing in a doorway at the far end of the apartment, wearing a suit even at 2 AM, holding a gold-plated Desert Eagle that looked like it belonged in a museum.

"You got balls," Trey said, aiming steady. "Stupid balls, but balls."

D Roc raised his AK.

They fired at the same time.

D Roc's burst went wide—Trey ducked back into the doorway. Trey's shot hit D Roc's body armor dead center, felt like getting hit by a car, knocked him backward into Tone.

"Fuck!" D Roc gasped, breath gone, ribs screaming.

Tone returned fire, long burst that chewed up the doorframe. Trey disappeared deeper into the apartment.

"We gotta go!" Tone said. "Cops gonna be here any second!"

"Not without his head!" D Roc struggled to his feet, ribs on fire but the armor had held. He pushed forward, into the hallway Trey had retreated down.

Bedroom at the end. Door closed. D Roc kicked it open—

Trey was at the window, gun still in hand, and for a split second their eyes met. There was no fear in Trey's face. Just cold calculation.

"You ain't special," Trey said. "You just another dead nigga who didn't know when to quit."

He fired. D Roc fired. Both missed.

Then Trey did something insane—he jumped. Through the window. Twenty stories up.

D Roc ran to the window and looked down, expecting to see a body on the pavement. Instead he saw a fire escape—narrow metal platform just below the window, leading down the side of the building.

Trey was already two floors down, moving fast.

"He's running!" D Roc yelled.

Sirens wailed in the distance. Close. Too close.

"We gotta go NOW!" Tone grabbed him. "Roc, we gotta—"

An explosion from the living room cut him off.

They ran back—smoke, fire, one of the bodyguards had thrown a grenade before dying, now the couch was burning, the curtains were burning, everything was burning.

"Shit! Shit! Shit!" Tone and D Roc bolted for the door, down the stairs, not caring about stealth anymore, just running, taking three steps at a time.

Nineteenth floor. Eighteenth. Seventeenth. They could hear cops entering the building below, voices shouting, boots pounding concrete.

"Service exit!" D Roc gasped, ribs screaming with every breath.

They hit the service entrance full speed, burst out into the alley, ripped off their masks. The van was where they left it. They threw the guns in back, jumped in front, D Roc driving, tires squealing as they pulled out.

Cop cars screamed past them going the other direction, toward the building, toward the fire, toward the bodies.

They drove. Fast but not crazy. Fast enough to get distance but not fast enough to attract attention.

Three blocks. Five. Ten. The Newark streets blurred past.

"Did we get him?" Tone asked, breathing hard. "Did you hit him?"

"I don't know. He went out the window, down a fire escape. I couldn't tell if he was hit or just running."

"Fuck!" Tone slammed his fist into the dashboard. "We went through all that and we don't even know if he's dead?"

D Roc's phone rang—the encrypted one. Carmen.

He put it on speaker.

"Is it done?" Carmen's voice was ice.

"I don't know. We hit the penthouse. Killed at least six bodyguards. Trey was there but he escaped through a window. I shot at him but—"

"But you don't have proof he's dead."

"No."

Silence. Long, terrible silence.

"Then you failed," Carmen said finally. "You had one job. Kill Trey Williams. You went in with everything I gave you and you failed."

"We can try again—"

"There is no 'again.' The building's on fire. The cops are everywhere. Trey's going to disappear now. Go to ground. You had your shot and you missed." Her voice dropped to something worse than anger—disappointment. "You have forty-eight hours. Either bring me proof Trey's dead, or I'm sending my people for you. Understood?"

"Carmen—"

"Forty-eight hours. Don't call me unless you have a body."

She hung up.

D Roc drove in silence, mind racing. They'd killed six people. Set a penthouse on fire. Caused a massive police response. And Trey was still alive. Somewhere in Newark, wounded or not, the man was still breathing.

Forty-eight hours. Two days to find a ghost in a city that wasn't his.

"We're dead," Tone said, staring out the window. "Even if we survive Carmen, even if we find Trey, we're dead. The cops got our faces on camera. They got our bullets. They got witnesses. We're dead."

D Roc didn't argue because Tone was right.

They were dead.

They just hadn't stopped moving yet.

They ditched the van in Harlem, burned it with everything inside—guns, body armor, masks. Let it all turn to ash and smoke.

D Roc walked back to the garage alone, every step agony, ribs purple with bruises where Trey's Desert Eagle round had hit the armor. Without the vest, he'd be dead. With it, he was just broken.

And he still owed Rodrigo a million dollars. That clock was ticking whether he was bleeding or not.

Inside the garage, he sat on the concrete floor, lit a Newport, and stared at nothing.

His phone buzzed. Not Carmen. Regular phone.

A news alert: *Breaking: Fatal shooting at Newark luxury building. Multiple casualties. Suspects fled. Police investigating.*

Another text. Unknown number.

Unknown: *Nice try, king. But you can't kill a ghost. See you soon. - Trey*

D Roc stared at the message, cigarette burning down to his fingers.

Trey was alive. Somewhere out there, planning his revenge. And D Roc had forty-eight hours to find him or die trying.

The phone buzzed again. This time a photo.

Tone. Standing outside a building D Roc recognized—Kenya's school. The photo was taken from across the street, telephoto lens, professional.

The message underneath: *Pretty little sister. Be a shame if something happened to her. Again.*

D Roc's blood went cold.

He called Tone immediately. "Get Kenya. Get your mom. Get somewhere safe. NOW."

"What's wrong?"

"Trey's coming for them. He sent me a photo. He knows where Kenya goes to school."

"Motherfucker!" Tone was already moving, D Roc could hear it. "I'm ten minutes away. I'll—"

Gunshots. Through the phone. Loud, rapid, automatic.

"Tone!" D Roc screamed into the phone. "Tone!"

Screaming. More gunshots. The sound of a phone hitting pavement.

Then silence.

"Tone! TONE!"

The line went dead.

D Roc tried calling back. Straight to voicemail. He tried again. Again. Again.

Nothing.

He sat there in the garage, holding a dead phone, knowing—just knowing—that his brother was gone.

Tone was dead.

Or dying.

Or captured.

And it was D Roc's fault.

All of it.

Every body.

Every death.

Every broken family.

His fault.

The crown fell off his head and shattered on the concrete.

He'd finally become exactly what Tasha said he was.

A monster.

CHAPTER TEN: ASHES

D Roc found Tone three hours later.

Not at Kenya's school. Not at his mama's house. At the spot where they'd first met fifteen years ago—a basketball court on 135th Street where kids used to hoop before the rims got stolen and never replaced.

Tone was slumped against the chain-link fence, head down, body still. Even from across the court, D Roc knew.

He ran anyway. Ran like maybe if he got there fast enough, Tone would still be breathing. Still be alive. Still be his brother.

But when D Roc dropped to his knees beside him, Tone's eyes were open and empty. Staring at nothing. Seeing nothing. Being nothing.

He'd been shot nine times. Chest, stomach, arms. They'd made sure. No chances. No mercy. Just execution.

Blood pooled under him, already drying in the cold morning air. His phone was next to his hand, screen cracked, last call still showing—D Roc's number.

He'd died calling for help that never came.

D Roc didn't scream. Didn't cry. Couldn't. All the tears had run out somewhere between Peezy and now. All that was left was a hollow space where his humanity used to live.

He closed Tone's eyes with shaking hands. "I'm sorry, brother. I'm so fucking sorry."

A piece of paper was pinned to Tone's chest with a knife. D Roc pulled it free, read the message written in blood—probably Tone's own blood.

"Your move, king. - Trey"

D Roc crumpled the note in his fist. Tone's body was the move. Tone's death was the message. Trey was telling him he could reach anyone, anywhere, anytime. That D Roc had nothing left to protect because everything he loved could be taken.

Sirens wailed in the distance. Someone had called 911. Probably heard the shots, waited a few minutes to make sure the shooters were gone, then called.

D Roc couldn't be here when the cops arrived. Couldn't answer questions. Couldn't explain why his best friend was dead on a basketball court with nine bullets in him.

"I'm gonna kill him," D Roc whispered to Tone's body. "I swear to God, I'm gonna kill him for this. For you. For Peezy. For Marcus. For all of it."

He stood, took one last look at his brother, and walked away.

Behind him, the sirens got louder.

Tone's mama found out by noon. D Roc heard her screaming from two blocks away when he went to check on Kenya. The sound was inhuman—the kind of wail that only comes from a mother who's lost her child. It echoed through the projects like a curse.

Kenya sat on the stoop, eyes dry, face blank. Thirteen years old and already dead inside. She'd been kidnapped, rescued, and now her brother was gone forever. That kind of trauma didn't heal. It just learned to hide.

"Miss Gloria," D Roc said quietly to Tone's mother when her screaming finally stopped. "I'm so sorry. I'm—"

She slapped him. Hard. The sound cracked like a gunshot.

"You!" she screamed, hitting him again. "This is your fault! My baby is DEAD because of you! Because you dragged him into your war! Because you couldn't just leave well enough alone!"

D Roc took the hits. Deserved them. Wanted more.

"You're the devil," Miss Gloria sobbed, collapsing against him even as she hit him. "You're death walking around in human skin. Everybody you touch dies. Everybody!"

Kenya finally looked up. Her voice was small, broken. "Why didn't you save him?"

The question hit harder than any slap.

"I tried—"

"You didn't try hard enough!" Kenya's voice cracked. "He was on the phone with you! He was calling for help and you didn't come! You let him die alone!"

"Kenya—"

"I hate you." She said it calm, matter-of-fact. Like she was commenting on the weather. "I hope whoever's trying to kill you succeeds. I hope you die the way my brother died. Alone. Scared. Calling for help that never comes."

She went inside. Miss Gloria followed, leaving D Roc standing on the stoop, drowning in guilt and grief and the weight of every death on his hands.

A kid on a bike rode past, looked at him, and spat. Word had already spread. D Roc was cursed. Death's best friend. The nigga you avoided if you wanted to live.

He pulled out a Newport, lit it with shaking hands, and smoked it down to the filter. Then lit another. And another. Chain-smoking until his lungs burned and his throat was raw and the pack was empty.

His phone buzzed. Carmen.

Carmen: *36 hours left. Where's my proof?*

He typed back: *I need more time. Trey killed my boy. I need—*

Carmen: *I don't care about your boy. I care about my contract. Trey dies in 36 hours or you do. Simple.*

D Roc: *He's underground. I can't find him.*

Carmen: *Then die looking. Clock's ticking.*

She didn't text again.

D Roc went to see Dre one last time.

The Bronx apartment was quiet. Shanice answered the door, eyes red from crying. She'd heard about Tone.

"He don't want to see you," she said.

"I know. But I gotta see him."

She let him in reluctantly.

Dre was on the couch, leg wrapped proper now—Shanice had gotten him to a doctor with the money D Roc gave her. He looked better physically. Worse in every other way.

"Come to collect my body?" Dre asked. "'Cause that's all you do now. Collect bodies."

"Dre—"

"Peezy's dead. Tone's dead. Marcus dead. Nova ran for his life. I'm next, ain't I? That's how this goes. Everybody around you dies until you're standing alone in a pile of corpses."

"I didn't want this."

"But you got it anyway." Dre struggled to sit up, winced. "You know what my mama said when I told her I'm leaving the game? She thanked Jesus. Actually got on her knees and thanked Jesus that her son might live past twenty-five. That's how bad it is, Roc. That's what we became. Dead men walking."

"I need help. One more time. Trey's out there and Carmen gave me thirty-six hours—"

"No."

"Dre—"

"I said NO!" Dre's voice cracked. "You don't get it, do you? I'm done dying for you. Done killing for you. Done being your soldier in a war you started. You wanna kill Trey? Do it yourself. You wanna settle with Carmen? That's on you. But leave me the fuck out of it."

"I can't do this alone."

"Then die." Dre looked him dead in the eyes. "Die, Roc. Because that's where this ends. That's the only way out. You die, or everybody around you does. Those are the options. So do us all a favor and just die already."

Shanice put a hand on Dre's shoulder. "Baby—"

"Nah." Dre shrugged her off. "He needs to hear it. Needs to understand. He ain't a king. He ain't a leader. He's a plague. And the best thing he could do for all of us is disappear."

D Roc stood there, taking it all in. Every word. Every truth. Every condemnation.

"You're right," he said finally. "About all of it."

He left without another word.

Outside, it started to rain. Cold October rain that felt like the city crying.

By nightfall, D Roc was drunk.

He'd bought a bottle of Hennessy from a bodega that didn't card and didn't care, and now he sat in the burned-out garage where this all started, drinking straight from the bottle, chain-smoking, staring at the weapons he didn't use and the armor that didn't save anyone.

His phone rang. Not Carmen. Not Trey. Tasha.

He almost didn't answer. What could he say to her? What words existed for this level of failure?

"Hello?"

"I heard about Tone." Her voice was thick with tears. "D, I'm so sorry. I know—I know he was like your brother."

"He was my brother."

"I know." She was crying openly now. "And I'm sorry. I'm so fucking sorry. For all of it. For leaving. For not being there. For—"

"Don't." D Roc took another pull from the bottle. "You were right to leave. You were smart. Everybody who stays around me dies. You got out before you became another body."

"That's not—"

"It's true." He laughed, but it was broken. "Peezy, Marcus, Tone—all dead. Nova ran away. Dre hates me. My whole crew is gone, Tasha. Everybody I ever cared about is either dead or wishes I was. And you know what? They're right.

I should die. The world would be better if I just put this gun in my mouth and—"

"Don't you dare." Her voice went hard. "Don't you fucking dare, D. You don't get to give up. You don't get to check out and leave me wondering if I could've saved you. If I could've—" She broke down completely. "Please. Please don't do nothing stupid. Just come see me. Let me hold you. Let me—"

"I can't. I got thirty-six hours to kill Trey or Carmen kills me. And even if I get Trey, there's Rodrigo's debt, and the cops, and the bounty, and all of it. There's no way out, baby. No door, no window, no escape. This is it. This is how it ends."

"Then let it end with me." She was begging now. "Come over. Right now. We'll have one more night. Just one. And tomorrow—tomorrow we'll figure it out together. Please, D. I can't lose you too."

He wanted to. God, he wanted to go to her, hold her, pretend for a few hours that they were normal people with normal problems. But he couldn't. Couldn't put that target on her. Couldn't risk Trey showing up and killing her the way he killed Tone.

"I love you," D Roc said. "More than anything in this world. And that's why I can't see you. Because if something happened to you because of me, I'd—I couldn't—"

"I'm already dying, D! Every day you're out there, every day I don't know if you're alive or dead, I'm dying! So just come home. Let me love you one more time. Let me—"

He hung up.

Couldn't listen anymore. Couldn't hear her beg. Couldn't feel her pain on top of his own.

He threw the phone across the garage. It shattered against the wall.

Then he drank more. And smoked more. And sat in the darkness wishing he'd never been born.

At 3 AM, clarity came through the drunken haze.

D Roc couldn't find Trey. Didn't know where he was hiding. Didn't have the resources to track him down.

But he knew where Trey would come eventually.

To him.

Trey wanted revenge. Wanted to kill D Roc personally. Prove he was the bigger man, the better killer, the real king.

So D Roc would give him the chance.

He pulled out the encrypted phone—the one Carmen gave him—and sent a message to every contact he could find. Let it spread through the streets like wildfire.

"D Roc challenges Trey Williams. Tomorrow night. Midnight. 118th Street. Just us. No crew. No backup. Winner takes all. Loser goes in the ground."

It was suicidal. Insane. Exactly what Trey wanted.

But it was the only play D Roc had left.

If Trey showed up, D Roc would kill him and maybe—MAYBE—survive Carmen's deadline.

If Trey didn't show up, D Roc would die anyway when Carmen's people came.

Either way, it ended tomorrow.

The phone buzzed almost immediately. Trey.

Trey: *You got balls, I'll give you that. Or you got a death wish. Either way, I'll be there. Midnight. 118th. Just you and me. No interference. May the best man win.*

D Roc: *Ain't about being the best. It's about being the last.*

Trey: *Same thing in our world.*

D Roc set the phone down and looked at his arsenal. One AK left. One .40. Body armor. And a whole lot of rage with nowhere left to go.

Tomorrow night, he'd put it all on 118th Street.

Tomorrow night, he'd either kill Trey Williams or die trying.

Tomorrow night would be the end.

One way or another.

He lit another Newport and watched the smoke curl toward the ceiling. Thought about Tone, about Peezy, about Marcus, about everyone who'd died for his pride.

Thought about Tasha, who loved a man who didn't deserve love.

Thought about the kid he used to be—the one who thought hustling was the way out, the way up, the way to something better.

That kid was dead.

Had been for a long time.

All that was left was D Roc.

And tomorrow night, maybe D Roc would be dead too.

The title finally made sense.

You can't be king of ashes.

You can't rule over graves.

You can't wear a crown made of guilt.

He smoked. He drank. He waited for tomorrow.

And prayed—to a God he didn't believe in—that when it was over, he'd at least take Trey with him.

At least then, it would mean something.

At least then, Tone wouldn't have died for nothing.

CHAPTER ELEVEN: THE LAST DAY

Friday morning came with rain and regret.

D Roc woke up on the garage floor, empty Hennessy bottle next to him, Newport butts scattered like shell casings. His head pounded. His ribs throbbed where Trey's bullet had hit the armor. His soul felt like something that had died and forgot to stop moving.

Today was the day.

Midnight. 118th Street. Him versus Trey.

One would walk away. One would be carried.

D Roc pulled himself up, every muscle screaming. He looked at his reflection in a piece of broken mirror leaning against the wall—hollow eyes, unshaven face, the look of a man who'd already died but his body hadn't gotten the message yet.

He looked like his father. The old man who'd drunk himself to death when D Roc was ten. The same empty eyes. The same defeated posture. History repeating itself in the worst possible way.

"Fuck that," D Roc muttered. He wouldn't die drunk. Wouldn't die weak. If this was his last day, he'd spend it getting right.

First: shower. He broke into an abandoned apartment on 142nd, used the cold water that still somehow ran, scrubbed off three days of death and desperation. Shaved with a rusty razor until his face was clean. Put on fresh clothes he'd stashed—black jeans, black hoodie, black Timbs. Dressed for a funeral. His own, probably.

Second: food. He hadn't eaten in two days. Found a bodega that wasn't asking questions, bought eggs and bacon and coffee. Ate it slow, tasting everything, knowing it might be his last meal. The bodega owner watched him like he knew D Roc was already a ghost.

Third: ammunition. He went to the garage, loaded every magazine he had left. The AK. The .40. Extra clips. He cleaned each weapon with ritual precision, treating them like the only friends he had left. Because they were.

By noon, he was ready to die.

But first, he had something to do.

Tone's funeral was at 2 PM.

D Roc knew he shouldn't go. Knew Miss Gloria would spit on him. Knew Kenya would scream. Knew the whole neighborhood would see him as the villain in this story.

But he had to. Had to say goodbye. Had to face what he'd done.

The funeral home was on Lenox, same place that had buried Peezy three days ago. Same place that would probably bury D Roc tomorrow if things went wrong tonight.

He stood outside in the rain, hood up, watching through the window. The casket was closed—Tone had been shot too many times for an open casket. Miss Gloria sat in the front row, Kenya next to her, both dressed in black, both destroyed.

The preacher talked about God's plan and better places and how Tone was with the angels now. But D Roc knew better. There were no angels for soldiers. Just dirt and darkness and the memory of what they used to be.

He didn't go inside. Couldn't. Just stood there in the rain, watching through glass, saying his own prayer to a God who'd stopped listening a long time ago.

"I'm sorry, brother," he whispered. "I'm sorry I got you killed. I'm sorry I dragged you into my war. I'm sorry for all of it. But I promise you—tonight I'm ending it. Tonight Trey dies. And maybe I die too. But at least it'll be over."

Someone touched his shoulder.

He spun, hand going to his .40—

It was Tasha.

She was soaked from the rain, makeup running, wearing a black dress and heels that looked wrong on a day this dark.

"I knew you'd be here," she said.

"You shouldn't be." He looked around, paranoid. "It's not safe. If Trey's people see you with me—"

"I don't care." She grabbed his face, made him look at her. "I don't care about Trey. I don't care about safe. I care about you. And if tonight's really it—if you're really going through with this insane plan—then I need to say something first."

"Tasha—"

"No. Listen." Tears mixed with rain on her face. "You're not a monster. I know I said you were. I know I blamed you for everything. But I was wrong. You're not a monster. You're just a man who got trapped in a situation he couldn't escape. And everything you did—every terrible thing—you did trying to survive. Trying to protect the people you love."

"That don't make it right."

"No. But it makes it human." She kissed him, soft and desperate. "Come home with me. Right now. Forget the challenge. Forget Trey. We'll run. We'll leave the city. We'll go somewhere they can't find us and we'll start over. Please, D. Please don't die tonight."

He wanted to say yes. Wanted to run away with her and never look back. But even as he thought it, he knew it was impossible. Carmen would hunt them. Rodrigo would hunt them. Trey would hunt them. There was no running anymore. Only forward, into the fire.

"I can't," he said, holding her close. "I gotta finish this. For Tone. For Peezy. For everyone who died because I wasn't strong enough to stop it earlier. But Tasha—" he pulled back, looked in her eyes, "—if I somehow survive tonight, I'm coming for you. We're leaving. Together. I promise."

"Don't make promises you can't keep."

"Then I won't promise. I'll just do it." He kissed her one more time, tasting her tears and the rain and everything he was about to lose. "I love you."

"I love you too." She clung to him. "Be smart tonight. Be careful. And if you get a chance to walk away—take it. Your pride ain't worth your life."

"I know."

He left her standing in the rain, watching him walk away, probably for the last time.

Inside the funeral home, someone started singing "Amazing Grace." The voice was old, weathered, beautiful in its pain.

D Roc walked toward his last day.

By 6 PM, 118th Street was a ghost town.

Word had spread fast. D Roc versus Trey. Midnight. Everyone who lived on the block either left for the night or locked their doors and prayed. Even the corner boys had disappeared. Nobody wanted to be anywhere near this.

D Roc stood in the middle of the street, smoking a Newport, looking at his kingdom. The block he'd fought for. Bled for. Killed for. It looked empty now. Meaningless. Just concrete and brick and broken dreams.

His phone buzzed. Carmen.

Carmen: *I'm told you challenged Trey to single combat. Dramatic. Stupid. But potentially effective. If you win, bring me his head. Literally. I want proof.*

D Roc: *If I win, we're done. No more contracts. No more jobs. I clear my debt and we're done.*

Carmen: *We'll see. Kill him first. Negotiate after.*

She didn't text again.

Another buzz. Rodrigo.

Rodrigo: *Heard about your showdown. You're either brave or suicidal. Either way, my money's still due in six months. Don't die tonight—I need you alive to collect.*

D Roc didn't respond. Rodrigo would get his money or he wouldn't. Either way, it wouldn't matter if D Roc was dead.

He checked his guns one more time. AK-47, fully loaded, safety off. .40 on his hip, extra clip. Body armor under his hoodie—the same vest that had saved him in Newark. Wouldn't save him twice, but it might buy him a second to shoot back.

At 9 PM, Detective Morrison showed up.

The cop pulled up in an unmarked sedan, got out slow, hands visible. No backup. No lights. Just a tired detective who'd seen too much death.

"Heard you got a war starting at midnight," Morrison said, standing twenty feet away. Professional distance.

"Heard right."

"Also heard Tone's funeral was today. And Peezy's was earlier this week. You're running out of friends real fast."

"I noticed."

Morrison sighed. "Look, D. I know you killed Bishop. I know you were in Newark Thursday night. I know you're in deep with the Colombians. And I know that tonight, you're either gonna kill Trey Williams or he's gonna kill you."

"So arrest me."

"Can't. Don't have enough evidence yet. Just enough to know you're dirty." Morrison took a step closer. "But here's the thing—I don't want to come back here tomorrow morning and find your body on this street. I don't want to call your girl and tell her you're dead. I don't want to add another Black kid to the pile of bodies this city produces."

"Then don't come back tomorrow."

"I have to. It's my job." Morrison looked at him with something like pity. "But I'm asking—man to man, not cop to criminal—walk away tonight. Let Trey go. Leave the city. Start over somewhere new. You're young. You're smart. You could still have a life."

"I had a life. I killed it."

"Then get a new one." Morrison handed him a card. "That's my personal number. If you change your mind before midnight, call me. I'll help you disappear. Witness protection, new identity, the works. But you gotta call before shots are fired. After that, I can't help you."

D Roc took the card, looked at it, put it in his pocket knowing he'd never call.

"Why you doing this?" D Roc asked. "Why you care?"

"Because I got a son your age." Morrison's voice went soft. "And every time I see a body on these streets, I see him. I see what he could become if he makes the wrong choices. So yeah, I care. Even about the ones I'm supposed to arrest."

Morrison got back in his car and drove away, leaving D Roc alone with his guns and his ghosts.

At 11 PM, someone unexpected showed up.

Dre. Limping on his bad leg, leaning on a cane, but armed with a nine millimeter on his hip.

"The fuck you doing here?" D Roc asked.

"Asking myself the same question." Dre limped closer. "I told you I was done. Told you to die alone. Meant every word."

"So why you here?"

"Because Tone would've been." Dre's voice cracked. "Because he would've stood by you even when you were wrong. Even when you were stupid. Even when you got him killed. He would've been here. So I'm here for him. Not for you. For him."

D Roc felt something in his chest unclench. "I can't ask you to fight."

"You didn't ask. I volunteered." Dre checked his nine, racked the slide. "Besides, Shanice kicked me out. Said if I wasn't man enough to help my brother, I wasn't man enough for her. So here I am. Being stupid with you one last time."

"You might die."

"We all die, Roc. Question is, do we die for nothing or do we die for something?" Dre positioned himself on the corner, using a stoop for cover. "Tonight we die for Tone. For Peezy. For Marcus. That's something."

D Roc nodded, not trusting himself to speak. One soldier. One last brother. It wasn't an army, but it was more than he deserved.

At 11:45, the block went dead silent. No cars. No voices. No music. Even the rats seemed to hide. The city held its breath.

At 11:58, headlights appeared at the end of 118th Street.

A black Escalade. Chrome rims. Jersey plates.

Trey.

The SUV stopped fifty feet away. Engine running. Lights on. Painting the street in harsh white glare.

The driver's door opened. Trey stepped out.

He looked just like he did in Newark—suit, gold Desert Eagle on his hip, cold eyes that had killed before and would kill again. Behind him, the Escalade held maybe four more soldiers. Armed. Ready.

"Thought you said one-on-one!" D Roc shouted.

"I lied!" Trey smiled. "Did you really think I'd play fair? You killed Bishop. You burned my money. You came to my home and tried to kill me. And you think I'm gonna respect some street code?"

The back doors of the Escalade opened. Four men got out. All strapped with AKs. All pointing at D Roc.

This wasn't a duel.

It was an execution.

"Last chance!" Trey called out. "Get on your knees. Beg for mercy. Maybe I'll make it quick."

D Roc looked at Dre. Dre looked back. They both knew this was it. Five against two. No escape. No backup. No way out but through.

"You ready?" D Roc asked.

"Nah," Dre said. "But let's do it anyway."

D Roc raised his AK.

Trey raised his Desert Eagle.

For one frozen moment, 118th Street held its breath.

Then someone yelled "NOW!" and the world exploded.

But the gunfire didn't come from Trey's crew.

It came from the rooftops.

Three shooters—rifles with scopes—opened up on the Escalade. Windows shattered. Tires exploded. One of Trey's soldiers dropped immediately, head shot. Another caught one in the chest, fell backward.

Trey dove behind his SUV. "What the fuck?!"

D Roc spun, trying to see who was shooting. The muzzle flashes came from three different rooftops around the block. Professional. Coordinated. Not his people.

Then he saw the shooters' silhouettes. Expensive gear. Tactical positioning.

Carmen's people.

She'd sent backup without telling him. Or she was making sure that whoever won tonight, she could control the outcome.

The firefight erupted into chaos.

Trey's remaining soldiers returned fire at the rooftops. D Roc and Dre lit up the Escalade, bullets punching through metal and glass. Trey shot back with his Desert Eagle, rounds hitting the pavement near D Roc's feet.

The street turned into a warzone. Smoke. Gunfire. Screaming. Blood.

One of Carmen's snipers took out another of Trey's soldiers. Two left, plus Trey.

Dre caught a round in his shoulder, spun, kept shooting through the pain. "I'm good! I'm good!"

D Roc changed magazines, popped up, fired controlled bursts. One of Trey's men went down. One left.

The last soldier made a run for it, trying to retreat to the Escalade. Carmen's sniper dropped him mid-stride.

Now it was just Trey. Pinned behind his shot-up SUV. Surrounded. Outgunned.

"Trey!" D Roc shouted. "It's over! Come out!"

"Fuck you!" Trey fired blind over the hood. "You brought the Colombians?! You that much of a bitch?!"

"I didn't bring nobody! They came on their own!"

"Bullshit!"

The snipers held their fire. Waiting. Watching.

D Roc approached the Escalade slow, AK up, finger on the trigger. Dre covered him from the corner, nine millimeter ready despite his bleeding shoulder.

"Last chance!" D Roc called. "Throw out your gun!"

Trey laughed. It sounded insane. "You really think you won? You think killing me changes anything? The Colombians own you now. They own your block. They own your whole fucking life. You ain't a king, D Roc. You're a slave."

"Maybe. But I'm a slave who's still breathing. Can you say the same?"

Trey stood up from behind the SUV. Desert Eagle in hand. Pointed at D Roc.

They both fired.

D Roc's AK barked three times. Center mass. Trey stumbled back, hit the Escalade, slid down leaving a red smear.

Trey's Desert Eagle went off once. The round hit D Roc's body armor again, same spot as Newark. The pain exploded through his chest. He dropped to one knee, gasping.

But he was alive.

Trey wasn't.

The Jersey kingpin slumped against his SUV, blood pooling, eyes going dim. He tried to speak. Couldn't. Tried to raise his gun. Couldn't.

Then he died.

Just like that. One second human, next second meat.

D Roc lowered his AK. Stood up slow. Walked to the body and looked down at the man who'd started this war.

"King of Nothing," D Roc said to the corpse. "Welcome to the club."

The snipers descended from the rooftops. Three Colombians in tactical gear. They approached Trey's body, one of them pulling out a phone and taking pictures. Proof for Carmen.

"She says good work," the lead sniper said in accented English. "You survived. That's rare."

"Am I free?" D Roc asked.

The sniper laughed. "Nobody's ever free. She'll call you when she needs you. Until then—" he gestured at the bodies, the blood, the destruction, "—enjoy your kingdom."

They left. Just disappeared into the night like they were never there.

D Roc stood in the middle of 118th Street, surrounded by corpses and shell casings and the ruins of everything he'd fought for.

Dre limped over, clutching his shoulder. "We won."

"Yeah." D Roc looked at the destruction. "We won."

It didn't feel like winning.

It felt like dying in slow motion.

Sirens wailed in the distance. Cops. Ambulances. The machinery of the city coming to clean up another mess.

"We gotta go," Dre said. "Before they get here."

D Roc looked at Trey's body one more time. Then at the street. His street. Bought with blood and death and everything he'd ever cared about.

"Yeah," he said. "Let's go."

They limped away together, leaving the dead behind, knowing tomorrow would bring more problems, more threats, more death.

But tonight?

Tonight they'd lived.

And sometimes, that was enough.

CHAPTER TWELVE: THE PRICE

They hid in an abandoned apartment on 145th Street while the sirens screamed through Harlem.

Dre was bleeding bad. The shoulder wound had opened up wider during their escape, and now blood soaked through his shirt, dripping onto the dusty floor. His face was gray, lips pale, breathing shallow.

"You need a hospital," D Roc said, trying to stop the bleeding with a torn bedsheet.

"Hospital means cops," Dre gasped. "Cops means jail. Jail means I'm dead anyway. Just—just wrap it tight and give me something for the pain."

D Roc had a half-bottle of Hennessy and a pack of Newports. That was it. He poured liquor on the wound—Dre screamed, bit down on a stick—then wrapped it as tight as he could. It wouldn't hold forever, but it might keep him alive until morning.

"Drink," D Roc said, handing him the bottle.

Dre drank deep, coughed, drank more. "We really did it. We really killed Trey."

"Yeah." D Roc lit a Newport, hands still shaking from adrenaline. "We did."

"So why don't it feel like winning?"

D Roc didn't have an answer. They sat in the darkness, listening to sirens, wondering if the cops would find them, wondering if Carmen's snipers were still watching, wondering what the fuck they were supposed to do now.

His phone buzzed. The encrypted one. Carmen.

Carmen: *Proof received. Trey Williams confirmed dead. Well done. Meet me at El Paraiso tomorrow. Noon. We discuss your future.*

D Roc: *Our deal was I kill Trey and we're done.*

Carmen: *The deal was you work for me until I say otherwise. Tomorrow. Noon. Don't be late.*

He threw the phone across the room. It bounced off the wall, didn't break, kept glowing with her message like a curse.

"She ain't letting you go, is she?" Dre asked.

"No."

"So we just traded one master for another. Trey's dead but we still slaves."

"Yeah." D Roc took a long drag, let the smoke burn his lungs. "That's exactly what we are."

By dawn, the news was everywhere.

D Roc's regular phone—the one he'd thought was shattered—still worked enough to pull up headlines. Every news site had the same story, different variations:

"Massacre on 118th Street: 5 Dead in Apparent Gang War"

"Harlem Bloodbath: Drug Dealer Trey Williams Among the Dead"

"NYPD Seeks Suspects in Friday Night Shooting"

The articles had details—too many details. Witnesses heard automatic gunfire. Forensics found shell casings from at least four different weapons. Security cameras caught partial footage of two men fleeing the scene. The Mayor was promising a crackdown. The Police Commissioner was calling it "domestic terrorism."

Detective Morrison was quoted: *"We know who's responsible. It's only a matter of time before we make arrests."*

They knew. They were coming.

"We gotta leave the city," Dre said, reading over his shoulder. "Like today. Right now. Before they pick us up."

"And go where? You think Carmen gonna let us just walk away? You think Rodrigo forgives a million-dollar debt because we changed zip codes?"

"So what, we just wait here to get locked up? Wait for the cops to kick down the door?"

"We go see Carmen. Get whatever money she owes us for Trey. Then we figure out the next move."

"The next move is Mexico. Or Canada. Or anywhere that ain't here." Dre struggled to stand, winced, fell back. "Fuck. I can't even walk straight. How I'm supposed to run?"

"You ain't. Shanice is gonna pick you up, take you to her aunt's house in Philly. You stay there until you heal. Until this dies down."

"And you?"

"I stay. I finish this."

"Finish what? It's already finished! We won! Trey's dead! The war's over!"

"The war ain't over till I say it is." D Roc crushed his cigarette on the floor. "Carmen wants me. Rodrigo wants his money. The cops want me in cuffs. I got three fights left and I ain't running from none of them."

"Then you're gonna die."

"Probably." D Roc pulled out his phone, texted Shanice with the address. "But at least I'll die on my feet."

Shanice picked up Dre at 8 AM, crying when she saw how much blood he'd lost, crying harder when he told her what they'd done. She helped him to her car, shot D Roc a look that said *this is your fault*, and drove away without a word.

D Roc was alone again.

He walked through Harlem in broad daylight, hood up, head down, just another nigga trying to be invisible in a city that saw everything. 118th Street was blocked off with yellow tape, cops everywhere, forensics teams taking pictures, news vans setting up for the noon broadcast.

His kingdom. His block. Now a crime scene.

He kept walking. Stopped at a bodega, bought more Newports, another bottle. The owner looked at him with knowing eyes, the kind that said *I know who you are and I ain't gonna say nothing but you need to leave.*

He left.

At 10 AM he called Tasha. It went to voicemail. He tried again. Voicemail. Again. Voicemail.

Finally texted: *I'm alive. Need to see you.*

Three dots appeared. Disappeared. Appeared again.

Tasha: *I can't. The police came to my apartment. Asked questions about you. About us. About where you were Friday night.*

D Roc: *What did you tell them?*

Tasha: *Nothing. But they're watching me now. Waiting for you to show up. If you come here, they'll arrest you.*

D Roc: *I need to see you. One more time.*

Tasha: *Then it'll be the last time. Is that what you want? For the last memory of us to be in handcuffs?*

He didn't respond. What could he say? She was right. The cops were probably tapping her phone. Probably had unmarked cars outside her building. Coming to her was suicide.

Tasha: *I love you. I'll always love you. But I can't be part of this anymore. I'm sorry.*

D Roc: *Don't be sorry. Be safe.*

Tasha: *You too.*

The conversation ended. So did they.

D Roc sat on a bench in Marcus Garvey Park, the same park where he'd confronted Bishop what felt like a lifetime ago. Smoked. Drank. Watched kids play basketball, old men play chess, women push strollers. Normal life. The kind he'd never have.

At 11:30, he headed to El Paraiso.

The restaurant was closed when he arrived, but the door was unlocked. Inside, Carmen sat at her usual table, wearing white this time—expensive pantsuit, gold jewelry, the look of a woman who'd never gotten her hands dirty because she paid people to do it for her.

Rodrigo was there too. And two of Carmen's soldiers, the kind with dead eyes and quick hands.

"Sit," Carmen said.

D Roc sat.

"Trey Williams is dead. You fulfilled your contract." Carmen slid an envelope across the table. "Two hundred thousand dollars as promised. Plus a bonus—fifty thousand—for the entertainment value. That shootout was spectacular. My people got excellent footage."

D Roc didn't touch the money. "We're done now. That was the deal."

"The deal was you work for me until I say otherwise." Carmen sipped her coffee, delicate and dangerous. "And I'm not saying otherwise. You're valuable, D Roc. You're effective. You get results. Why would I let that go?"

"Because I'm done killing for you."

"Are you?" She smiled. "Because I have another job. Easy one. Barely qualifies as work."

"I said I'm done."

"And I said you're not." Her smile vanished. "You belong to me. You accepted my money. You used my weapons. You killed for me. That makes you mine. And the only way you stop being mine is when you're dead. So unless you'd like me to arrange that right now—" she gestured to her soldiers, "—I suggest you listen to the job."

D Roc's hand drifted toward his .40. The soldiers' hands mirrored the movement. Three guns would be out before he could draw. He'd be dead before he hit the floor.

"Smart choice," Carmen said. "Now. The job. There's a witness. A young man who saw things he shouldn't have seen. Things about my operation. Things that could cause problems if he talks to the wrong people. I need him silenced."

"I ain't killing no witness."

"Not killing. Just... convincing. Scare him. Make sure he understands that talking is bad for his health. Think you can do that without shooting anyone?"

D Roc looked at Rodrigo, who'd been silent this whole time. "You got something to say?"

"I got a million dollars to collect in six months," Rodrigo said. "You do what Carmen needs, she pays you, you pay me. Everybody wins. You refuse—" he shrugged, "—we all lose. Especially you."

D Roc was trapped. Completely, utterly trapped. He'd killed Trey thinking it would free him, but all it did was tighten the chains.

"Where's the witness?" D Roc asked.

Carmen smiled. "See? I knew you'd be reasonable." She slid a photo across the table. A kid, maybe seventeen, wearing a college hoodie, smiling at the camera like he had a future.

"His name is Marcus Rodriguez. College student. Wrong place, wrong time. Saw a shipment he shouldn't have seen. Lives in Washington Heights with his grandmother. Address is on the back of the photo."

D Roc stared at the kid's face. Looked like Marcus—his Marcus, the one who'd burned alive. Same age. Same innocence. Same doomed future.

"When?" D Roc asked.

"Tonight. Before he decides to talk to police. My people will be watching to make sure you do it right." Carmen stood, smoothed her suit. "Oh, and D Roc? Don't try to run. Don't try to warn him. Don't try to be a hero. Just do the job. Scare the kid. Come back. Collect your money. That's it."

She left with her soldiers.

Rodrigo stayed behind. "You look like shit," he said.

"I feel worse."

"Good. That means you're still human." Rodrigo lit a cigar. "You know what the worst part of this life is? Not the killing. Not the drugs. Not even the prison time. It's the realization that you're never getting out. That every choice you made led you deeper into a hole you can't climb out of."

"Then why you still in it?"

"Because I'm too old to learn a new trade." He blew smoke. "But you? You're young. You could still walk away. Disappear. Start over."

"Carmen said—"

"Carmen says a lot of things. But between you and me? You don't belong to her. You belong to yourself. You just gotta decide what that means." Rodrigo stood, left money on the table for coffee Carmen didn't pay for. "Do the job or don't. Either way, my money's still due."

He left.

D Roc sat alone in the empty restaurant, staring at a photo of a kid who didn't deserve to die but probably would anyway, holding an envelope of blood money that wouldn't save him, smoking a cigarette that tasted like failure.

His phone buzzed. News alert.

"Police Identify Suspects in 118th Street Massacre: Warrants Issued"

He clicked the link. His face was there. Not a good photo—pulled from old surveillance footage, grainy, but recognizable. The caption: *"Darrell 'D Roc' Roc, wanted for questioning in multiple homicides."*

They had his government name. His face. Warrants.

It was over.

Even if he ran, they'd find him. Even if he killed Marcus Rodriguez, more jobs would come. Even if he paid Rodrigo, Carmen would own him forever.

There was no winning.

There was no escape.

There was just this—sitting in an empty restaurant, smoking cigarettes, holding blood money, staring at a photo of a kid he was supposed to terrorize tonight.

He finally understood what it meant.

You could have power. You could have money. You could have respect.

But if you had no freedom, no love, no future—you had nothing.

And D Roc had nothing.

He picked up the envelope of money. Two hundred and fifty thousand dollars. Enough to pay Rodrigo and have plenty left over. Enough to run somewhere far away. Enough to start over.

Or enough to buy one last act of defiance.

He made a choice.

At 6 PM, D Roc stood outside the apartment building in Washington Heights where Marcus Rodriguez lived with his grandmother.

Through the window on the third floor, he could see movement. A shadow passing. The kid was home. Probably doing homework. Probably thinking about college applications and a future that still looked possible.

D Roc thought about another Marcus. Lil Marcus. The sixteen-year-old who burned alive because D Roc put him in a building full of product. The kid who wanted to get his moms out the projects. The kid whose mama had told D Roc to make it right.

"Don't try. Do."

Her words echoed in his head. All those deaths—Peezy, Tone, Lil Marcus—they couldn't mean nothing. They couldn't just be bodies in a pile. There had to be something he could save. Someone he could keep from becoming another ghost.

He didn't go inside.

Instead, he slipped an envelope under the door—fifty thousand dollars in cash and a note written on the back of Carmen's photo:

"They're coming for you. Take your grandmother and run. Don't tell anyone where. Don't look back. This money will get you started somewhere new. Don't waste it. Don't come back. Live. Live for all the kids who didn't get the chance."

Then he walked away.

Carmen's watchers were out there somewhere. He could feel their eyes on him. They'd report back that he warned the kid instead of scaring him. They'd tell Carmen he defied her.

And she'd send people to kill him.

But for the first time in weeks, D Roc felt something other than guilt or rage or despair.

He felt human again.

Even if it only lasted until Carmen found out.

Even if it got him killed tomorrow.

For tonight, he'd saved one kid instead of destroying him. One Marcus instead of losing another.

For tonight, he wasn't King of Nothing.

He was just Darrell.

And maybe that was enough.

CHAPTER THIRTEEN: HUNTED DOGS

Carmen found out in less than four hours.

D Roc was in a motel on the edge of the Bronx—the kind where you paid cash and the clerk didn't look at your face—when the encrypted phone rang at 10 PM.

He knew before he answered.

"You disobeyed me," Carmen said. No anger. Just cold statement of fact

"Yeah."

"I told you to scare the witness. You gave him money and told him to run. My watchers saw everything."

"Good for them."

"Do you understand what you've done?" Still calm. That was worse than screaming. "You've shown me you can't be trusted. You've shown me you're weak. Sentimental. Those are liabilities I can't afford."

D Roc lit a Newport, blew smoke at the stained ceiling. "So what you gonna do? Kill me?"

"Eventually. But first, I'm going to make sure you understand the cost of defiance." She paused. "I know where Dre is. Philadelphia. His girlfriend's aunt's house. 2847 North Broad Street. Nice neighborhood. Quiet. Safe."

D Roc's blood went cold. "You leave him out of this."

"But he's part of this. He helped you kill Trey. He helped you defy me. So he pays too." Carmen's voice was ice. "I'm sending people. They'll be there in an hour. Unless—"

"Unless what?"

"Unless you do what you should've done in the first place. Marcus Rodriguez is still in Washington Heights. Find him. Kill him. Bring me proof. Then maybe—MAYBE I'll call off my people before they get to Philadelphia."

"He's already gone. I gave him money to run."

"Then you better hope he didn't run far." Carmen hung up.

D Roc stared at the phone, mind racing. She was going to kill Dre. Going to kill an innocent kid. All because D Roc tried to do one decent thing.

He called Dre immediately.

"Yeah?" Dre sounded groggy, probably sleeping off painkillers.

"You need to leave. Right now. Carmen knows where you are. She's sending people."

"What? How—"

"Doesn't matter how. Get Shanice, get her aunt, get the fuck out of there. Right now. Don't pack. Just run."

"Roc, I can barely walk—"

"Then crawl! They're coming!" D Roc was already moving, grabbing his gun, his keys. "I'm on my way but I'm an hour out. You got maybe thirty minutes. MOVE!"

He hung up, ran to the stolen car he'd been using, peeled out of the motel parking lot. Philadelphia was forty-five minutes if he drove like hell.

He drove like hell.

The highway blurred past. D Roc pushed the car to ninety, weaving through traffic, one hand on the wheel, other hand on his .40. His phone rang constantly—Dre calling back, panicking. D Roc didn't answer. He needed to focus. Needed to drive.

Carmen's people would be professionals. Fast. Efficient. Deadly.

Dre was wounded, slow, with two civilians. He wouldn't make it out unless—

Unless D Roc got there first.

He pushed the car to a hundred. The engine screamed. The whole vehicle shook. He didn't care.

At 10:47 PM, he hit Philadelphia.

At 10:53, he was on North Broad Street.

At 10:55, he saw the house—2847, brick row home, lights on, a Honda in the driveway. Dre's shadow moving past the window. Still inside. Still alive.

D Roc parked two houses down, grabbed his gun, approached on foot. His phone buzzed. Text from Dre.

Dre: *Where are you???*

D Roc: *Outside. Don't come out yet. Let me check.*

He moved quiet, scanning the street. Three cars that didn't belong—too new, too clean for this neighborhood. Empty. Engines still warm.

Carmen's people were already here.

"Fuck," D Roc whispered.

He tried the front door. Locked. He went around back, found a basement window, forced it open, dropped inside into darkness. The basement smelled like mildew and old laundry. Stairs led up to the first floor.

He could hear voices upstairs. Calm. Professional. Spanish.

"—encontrarlos. Tres personas. Uno está herido—"

"—the girl first. She'll tell us where they ran—"

D Roc crept up the stairs, gun raised. The kitchen door was open. He could see through to the living room. Two men—Colombians, tactical gear, suppressed pistols. One had Shanice on her knees, gun to her head. The other was searching the house.

Where was Dre?

Where was Shanice's aunt?

A floorboard creaked above him. The second Colombian turned toward the stairs leading to the second floor—

D Roc shot him twice in the back. The suppressed .40 made two soft coughs. The man dropped.

The first Colombian spun, dragging Shanice up as a shield, gun pointed at D Roc—

Dre came down the stairs behind him, moving silent despite his bad leg, and put his nine millimeter to the Colombian's head.

"Drop it," Dre said.

The Colombian didn't. Tried to spin and shoot—

Dre shot him in the temple. The man collapsed, taking Shanice down with him.

She screamed. Kept screaming. Couldn't stop.

"Where's your aunt?" Dre asked, helping her up.

"Closet—I hid her in the closet—"

"Get her. We're leaving. Now."

D Roc checked the bodies. Dead. But there were three cars outside. Three.

"Where's the third one?" D Roc asked.

Gunfire answered. From upstairs. The third Colombian—up there, shooting, trying to flush them out.

"Back door!" Dre grabbed Shanice, pushed her toward the kitchen. "Go! Go!"

They ran. D Roc covered them, firing up the stairs, keeping the Colombian pinned. Wood splintered. Plaster exploded. The whole house shook with gunfire.

Outside, Shanice got her aunt—old woman, terrified, confused—into the Honda. Dre jumped in the driver's seat despite his shoulder, started the engine.

D Roc emptied his magazine up the stairs, backed toward the door—

The Colombian came down firing. Round caught D Roc in the thigh. He went down, pain exploding through his leg.

Dre screamed his name.

D Roc fired his last rounds from the floor. Hit the Colombian twice. The man stumbled, fell down the stairs, landed in a heap.

Not moving.

"ROC!" Dre was out of the car, limping back toward the house.

"I'm good! Go! Get them out of here!" D Roc dragged himself toward the door, blood pouring from his leg. "GO!"

Dre hesitated one second, then jumped back in the Honda and burned rubber getting away.

D Roc crawled out the back door, fell down the steps, landed in the yard. His leg was on fire. The bullet had gone clean through—in the front, out the back—but it hurt like nothing he'd ever felt.

Sirens. Cops coming. Neighbors calling 911.

He had to move.

Had to get up.

Had to run.

He pulled himself up using the fence, hobbled to the alley, found his stolen car two blocks over, nearly passed out getting in.

Drove away as cop cars screamed past toward the house.

He made it back to New York somehow. Don't remember the drive. Just pain and blood and trying not to crash.

By 2 AM he was in an abandoned building on 152nd Street, using a first aid kit he'd bought at a 24-hour CVS, trying to patch his leg. The bullet hole went straight through the meat of his thigh—missed the bone, missed the artery, but hurt like hell and bled like a faucet.

He poured alcohol on it—screamed into his fist—wrapped it tight with gauze and tape. It wouldn't hold long but it might keep him alive until morning.

His phone rang. Not Carmen. Detective Morrison.

He answered. Why not? What did it matter anymore?

"Yeah?"

"We know what happened in Philadelphia." Morrison's voice was tired. Disappointed. "Three bodies. Colombian nationals. House shot to pieces. And blood in the alley—your blood type, I'm guessing."

"You guessing or you know?"

"I know. We got your DNA from 118th Street. Matched it to evidence in Newark. Matched it to Philadelphia." Morrison sighed. "D Roc, this is your last chance. Turn yourself in. Right now. We'll protect you. Witness protection. New life. But you gotta come in before more people die."

"Can't do that."

"Why not?"

"Because I'm already dead. I'm just waiting for my body to figure it out."

"Don't talk like that. You're young. You can still—"

"I can still what? Get life in prison? Get killed by Carmen's people in lockup? Get buried in an unmarked grave somewhere? Nah, Detective. I'm good. But I appreciate you trying."

"D Roc—Darrell—"

He hung up.

Sat there bleeding, smoking, staring at nothing.

His phone buzzed. Carmen.

Carmen: *You killed my people. Three professionals. Expensive professionals. You're going to pay for that. In blood.*

D Roc: *Get in line. Everybody wants me dead.*

Carmen: *The difference is, I have the resources to make it happen. You have 24 hours. Then I send everyone. Every soldier. Every asset. Every resource. And I don't just kill you. I kill everyone you've ever cared about. Tasha. Dre. Shanice. Her aunt. Everyone.*

D Roc: *Tasha left me. She's not part of this.*

Carmen: *She was in love with you. That makes her part of it. 24 hours. Use them wisely.*

She didn't text again.

D Roc looked at his leg, his gun, his empty pack of cigarettes. He was out of smokes, out of bullets, out of time.

24 hours.

One day left to live.

He laughed. It sounded insane. Maybe he was.

His phone rang again. Unknown number. He answered out of curiosity.

"Yeah?"

"D Roc?" A young voice. Male. Scared.

"Who this?"

"Marcus. Marcus Rodriguez. The kid—the one you saved. You gave me money and told me to run."

D Roc sat up straight. "How'd you get this number?"

"It was on the envelope. You wrote it on the back of the note." Marcus's voice cracked. "I just—I wanted to say thank you. I wanted to tell you that you saved my life. Me and my abuela—we're in Boston now. Far away. Safe. Because of you."

D Roc felt something in his chest unclench. Just a little. Just enough to remind him he was still human.

"You stayed safe, yeah?" D Roc asked.

"Yes sir. We left that night. Took a bus. Paid cash. We're not coming back. Ever."

"Good. Don't. Don't even tell me where exactly you are. Just live. Be a good kid. Go to college. Make something of yourself."

"I will. I promise. And Mr. D Roc? I don't know why you saved me. I don't know what kind of trouble you're in. But whatever it is—thank you. Thank you for being the one good thing in whatever bad stuff is happening."

The kid hung up.

D Roc thought about Nova then—the kid with the camera who'd filmed everything before he got out. Nova had said he destroyed the footage like D Roc ordered, but there was something in his voice when he said it. Like maybe he kept copies. Like maybe somewhere there was a record of everything that happened, waiting to tell the truth someday.

D Roc hoped Nova was smart enough to keep it hidden. And maybe someday, when all the players were dead or locked up, that footage would matter. Would show what really happened on these streets. Would be the evidence that survived when the witnesses didn't.

But that was a problem for another day. If there was another day.

D Roc sat there holding a dead phone, tears running down his face.

One good thing.

In an ocean of blood and death and destruction, he'd done one good thing.

Marcus was alive. In Boston. Safe. Because D Roc chose humanity over orders.

Maybe that was worth dying for.

Maybe that made all the other deaths mean something.

Maybe—

His phone buzzed again. This time a photo.

Tasha. Walking into her apartment building. From today. Recent.

The message underneath: 24 hours. - Carmen

D Roc's tears stopped. The grief turned to rage. Cold. Focused. Murderous.

Carmen wanted war?

He'd give her war.

One last war.

He pulled himself up, leg screaming. Hobbled to the bathroom, found a needle and thread in his kit, and stitched his own leg closed. No anesthetic. Just pain and rage and determination.

Twenty minutes later, the leg was stitched, wrapped, and functional. Barely.

He loaded his last magazine. Seven rounds. That was all he had left.

Seven rounds and 24 hours.

It would have to be enough.

He made a list in his head of everyone who needed to die before he did:

1. Carmen Vasquez. 2. Her soldiers. 3. Anyone between him and her.

Rodrigo wasn't on the list. The detective wasn't on the list. The cops weren't on the list.

Just Carmen.

Just the Colombian bitch who thought she owned him.

By tomorrow night, one of them would be dead.

D Roc was betting on her.

He found a payphone—one of the last working ones in Harlem—and made a call.

"El Paraiso restaurant," a voice answered.

"Tell Carmen I'm coming for her. Tomorrow. Noon. Same place we met. Just me and her. No soldiers. No backup. She wants me dead? Come get me yourself."

"Sir, I don't know what—"

"She'll know. Tell her." D Roc hung up.

He limped back to his stolen car, got in, drove to a spot where he could see Tasha's building. Parked across the street. Watched her window. Made sure no one approached.

He'd guard her tonight. One last act of love.

Tomorrow, he'd end this.

One way or another.

But at least he'd die on his feet.

At least he'd die fighting.

At least Marcus Rodriguez was alive in Boston, safe, with a future.

And maybe—just maybe—that was enough.

CHAPTER FOURTEEN: NO EXIT

The rain started Tuesday morning and didn't stop for three days.

D Roc watched it from a motel window on the edge of Queens, smoking Newports and drinking cheap whiskey because the Hennessy ran out and he couldn't risk going to a liquor store where somebody might recognize him. His face was all over the news. Not his name—not yet—but security footage from Newark. Grainy shit, masks and body armor, but the cops were calling it "the Harlem crew" and Detective Morrison was on TV every night talking about "imminent arrests."

Imminent meant soon. Imminent meant they knew.

His phone—the regular one, not Carmen's encrypted bullshit—had forty-seven missed calls from numbers he didn't recognize. Reporters. Cops pretending to be friends. People trying to collect the bounty Trey had put out before he died.

The bounty was still active. Nobody told Trey's people to call it off. So now D Roc had killed the man and still had a million-dollar target on his back.

He crushed out his cigarette and lit another. The pack was almost empty. Everything was almost empty. Money, crew, hope.

The encrypted phone buzzed. Carmen.

He let it ring four times before answering. Small act of defiance that would probably get him killed.

"You're late," Carmen said.

"Late for what?"

"El Paraiso. Noon. I said noon yesterday. It's now Wednesday."

"I been laying low. Cops everywhere."

"That's not my problem." Her voice was ice wrapped in silk. "We had a meeting. You missed it. That's disrespectful."

"The contract's done. I killed Trey. We're square."

Silence. Long, dangerous silence.

"Square?" Carmen laughed, but it wasn't a sound that contained joy. "You think killing two people makes us square? You think that clears your debt to me?"

"That was the deal. Bishop and Trey. I delivered both."

"The deal was you work for me until I say you're done. And I'm not done with you."

D Roc stood up, paced the small room. "Nah. Nah, that ain't—we had a contract. Specific terms. I held up my end."

"You held up the minimum. Now I'm exercising my option for additional services." Carmen's voice went cold. "You're an asset, D Roc. A useful tool. And I don't throw away useful tools just because they completed one job."

"I ain't your tool."

"You became my tool the moment you accepted my money. The moment you killed Bishop in that barbershop. The moment you realized you couldn't survive without me." She paused. "You owe Rodrigo a million dollars. You have cops building a murder case. You have bounty hunters trying to collect Trey's reward. You need protection. Resources. Money. I provide all of that. In exchange, you do what I tell you."

"And if I refuse?"

"Then I stop protecting you. I tell Rodrigo where you are. I tell the cops where you are. I tell every bounty hunter in the tristate area where you are. How long do you think you'd survive? A day? An hour?"

D Roc's hand shook as he brought the cigarette to his lips. She was right. She was absolutely right. He was trapped. Had been trapped since the moment he shook her hand at that restaurant.

"What do you want?" he asked quietly.

"That's better. El Paraiso. Tomorrow. Don't be late again."

She hung up.

D Roc threw the phone at the wall. It bounced, didn't break, just lay there glowing with her contact info like a curse that wouldn't end.

He needed to get out. Needed to run. Mexico, maybe. Or Canada. Somewhere Carmen's reach didn't extend.

But her reach extended everywhere. That's what made her dangerous. She had cops on payroll, politicians in her pocket, soldiers in every major city. Running from her was just dying slowly in a different location.

His regular phone buzzed. Unknown number. He almost didn't answer.

"Yeah?"

"Mr. Roc?" A man's voice. Formal. Professional.

"Who this?"

"My name is Detective Morrison. NYPD Homicide. I think we should talk."

D Roc's blood went cold. "I got nothing to say to you."

"I think you do. See, I know you killed Marcus Hayes—Bishop. I know you were involved in the Newark massacre. I know you're responsible for at least six deaths in the past month. And I know you're running out of places to hide."

"You got evidence, come arrest me."

"I'm working on that. But here's the thing—I don't care about you. You're a symptom. I care about the disease." Morrison's voice softened slightly. "Carmen Vasquez. The Colombian cartel. The real players who're flooding our streets with poison and turning young men like you into killers. Help me get them, and maybe we can work something out."

"Work something out?" D Roc laughed bitterly. "You mean snitch? Rat out the people who'll kill me and everyone I ever knew if I flip?"

"I mean survive. Because right now, you're a dead man. Carmen's using you. When she's done, she'll throw you away like garbage. At least with us, you'd have witness protection. A new identity. A chance at a real life."

"I don't snitch."

"Then you die. It's that simple." Morrison sighed. "Look, I've been doing this twenty-three years. I've seen hundreds of guys like you. Smart. Loyal. Trying to do right by their crew. And you know where they all ended up? Prison or the morgue. That's it. Those are the only two options for people in your position."

"There's a third option."

"What's that?"

"I figure this shit out myself."

D Roc hung up.

He sat there, phone in hand, realizing Morrison was probably right. Prison or the morgue. Those were the options. Had always been the options. The game didn't have happy endings. Never did.

Another cigarette. Another pull from the bottle. The rain kept falling.

By Thursday morning, D Roc was broke.

Not struggling. Not low on funds. Actually broke. He'd been living off Carmen's money—the $150K she'd paid him for Bishop—but that was almost gone. Motels, food, new phones every other day, payments to people for fake IDs and safe houses. Money disappeared fast when you were running.

He needed to get paid again. Which meant going to see Carmen. Which meant walking into whatever trap she'd set.

No choice. Never any choices.

El Paraiso looked different in daylight. Less elegant, more tired. The paint was chipping. The awning had a hole in it. Funny how everything looked better at night when you couldn't see the decay.

The same hostess from before—young, pretty, terrified—led him through the empty restaurant to the back office. Carmen was waiting, sitting behind her desk like a queen on a throne. She looked tired too. Or maybe that was just D Roc projecting.

"Sit," she said.

He sat.

Carmen poured two glasses of whiskey, slid one across. "You look terrible."

"Feel worse."

"Good. Suffering builds character." She took a sip. "I have work for you."

"What kind of work?"

"There's a man. Haitian. Runs a crew out of Brooklyn. He's been stepping on my territory, moving product without permission. I want him gone."

"Gone like scared away or gone like dead?"

"What do you think?"

D Roc stared at his glass. "I ain't a hitman."

"You killed Bishop. You killed Trey. You killed six bodyguards in Newark. What would you call that?"

"Survival. Self-defense. War."

"Call it whatever helps you sleep." Carmen leaned forward. "This is the new arrangement. I give you jobs. You complete them. I pay you and keep you protected. Simple."

"For how long?"

"Until you're no longer useful. Or until you die. Whichever comes first."

"And my debt to Rodrigo?"

"Still yours. But I can help you manage it. Make payments on your behalf in exchange for services." She smiled. "Think of me as your employer now. A very generous employer who keeps you alive and out of prison."

D Roc lit a Newport, blew smoke at her ceiling. "What if I refuse?"

"We've been over this. You don't get to refuse." Carmen's voice went flat. "But let me make it clearer. If you walk out that door without accepting this arrangement, my people will kill you before you reach your car. If you try to run, I'll find you. If you try to hide, I'll burn down every place you've ever felt safe. I own you now, D Roc. The sooner you accept that, the easier this gets."

The rain kept falling outside. The restaurant was quiet except for kitchen sounds—pots clanging, somebody yelling in Spanish.

"How much?" D Roc asked finally.

"For the Haitian? Fifty thousand."

"That's less than you paid for Bishop."

"Bishop was a threat to my operation. The Haitian's just an annoyance. Value scales with importance." Carmen pulled out a folder, slid it across. "His name's Bertrand. Photo, addresses, known associates. He runs a nightclub in Bed-Stuy. Easy target."

D Roc opened the folder. The man inside was maybe forty, dreadlocks, gold teeth, mean eyes. Another hustler trying to make it. Another body waiting to happen.

"When?"

"This week. Saturday latest."

"And after?"

"After, there'll be someone else. And someone after that. And someone after that." Carmen finished her whiskey. "This is your life now. Accept it or die fighting it. Those are your options."

D Roc closed the folder. "What about the cops? Morrison's building a case."

"Let him build. He has no witnesses, no physical evidence tying you to anything. The security footage from Newark is grainy. The Bishop murder has no surveillance. You're smart enough not to leave DNA." Carmen waved her hand dismissively. "Morrison's desperate. Grasping. He'll never make a case stick."

"He offered me a deal. Witness protection if I flip on you."

Carmen's expression didn't change. "And what did you tell him?"

"Told him I don't snitch."

"Good. Because if you had told him anything else, you'd already be dead." She stood up, signaling the meeting was over. "Saturday. The Haitian. Don't make me send people to motivate you."

D Roc stood too, pocketed the folder. "I want half up front."

"You want a lot of things. You'll get paid when it's done."

"Half up front or I walk."

Carmen studied him for a long moment. Then she opened a drawer, pulled out a stack of bills, counted out twenty-five thousand. "Half now. Half on proof of death. And D Roc? Don't test me again. My patience has limits."

He took the money, turned to leave.

"One more thing," Carmen said. "Your friend Dre. The one in Philadelphia. He's been talking. Nothing specific yet, but he's been seen with people who ask too many questions. If he becomes a problem, he becomes your problem. Understand?"

D Roc's jaw tightened. "He won't talk."

"Make sure of it."

Outside, the rain had finally stopped. The city smelled like wet concrete and exhaust fumes. D Roc sat in his car—a different stolen Honda, this one blue—and counted the money. Twenty-five thousand. Enough to survive a few more weeks. Enough to keep running a little longer.

But not enough to escape.

There was no escape. Carmen made that clear. He was hers now. A slave with a long leash but a slave nonetheless.

His phone buzzed. Regular phone. Rodrigo.

"We need to talk," Rodrigo said without preamble.

"About what?"

"Your debt. You owe me a million dollars. Six months, we agreed. It's been two months. I want to see a payment plan."

"I'm working on it."

"Working on it isn't cash in my hand. I want fifty thousand by next Friday. Call it a good faith payment."

"I don't have fifty thousand."

"Then get it. Rob someone. Kill someone. I don't care. But if I don't see money next week, I start taking things you care about." Rodrigo's voice was calm, matter-of-fact. "Your territory. Your connect. Eventually your life. Business is business."

He hung up.

D Roc sat there, phone in hand, doing math that didn't work. Carmen just gave him twenty-five thousand. After he killed the Haitian, he'd get another twenty-five. Fifty total. Which he owed to Rodrigo. Which meant he'd be right back at zero.

Broke. Trapped. Working for Carmen to pay Rodrigo to stay alive long enough to work for Carmen again.

The crown had finally become a noose.

He lit another Newport, started the car, and drove. Nowhere specific. Just drove. Through Queens, through Manhattan, across the bridge into Harlem. Past 118th Street, which was still blocked off with crime scene tape. Past the spot where Peezy died. Past the basketball court where he found Tone's body.

Ghosts everywhere. Every corner held a memory of someone who didn't make it. Every block was a graveyard disguised as a neighborhood.

His phone buzzed again. This time a text. Unknown number.

Unknown: *I'm pregnant. We need to talk. - Tasha*

D Roc stared at the message until the words stopped making sense. Read it again. Again. Like maybe the letters would rearrange themselves into something that didn't feel like a knife in his chest.

Pregnant.

He thought about his mama. How she'd raised him alone after his pops got locked up. How she'd worked two jobs and still couldn't keep him from the streets. How she'd cried when she found his first gun and he'd promised her he'd be different.

He wasn't different. He was exactly what she'd feared.

And now there was gonna be another kid. Another life. Another person who'd have to answer for his sins.

D Roc pulled over, turned off the car, and cried for the first time since Tone died. Not quiet tears. Real crying. The kind that comes from somewhere deeper than grief. The kind that says everything you thought you knew about yourself was a lie.

Because now there was something else to lose.

Something innocent.

Something that didn't deserve the life he was about to give it.

He sat there until the tears stopped and his face went numb. Then he lit a Newport with shaking hands and watched the smoke curl toward the ceiling like a prayer that wouldn't reach God.

And now, maybe, father of nothing too.

* * *

She didn't tell anybody.

That was the first decision. Before the clinic, before the appointment, before any of it. Tasha sat in her bathroom on the closed toilet seat with the test stick on the edge of the sink and watched the second blue line bloom like a bruise, and she made up her mind: nobody was gonna know but her.

Not her mama, who'd lived in Mount Vernon for nineteen years and still talked to her like she was twelve. Not her sister Diane down in Maryland, just had her second baby and had opinions about everything. Not Keisha at the salon, who told everybody everything two minutes after she heard it. Not even the girls she'd grown up with on 116th, who would smile to her face and put her on the phone tree before she made it home.

This was hers. This problem. This decision. This cell-cluster the size of a peppercorn that had her grandmother's wide hips and D Roc's stubborn jaw waiting inside it.

She made the appointment from the phone she only used for the salon. Manhattan, not Harlem—she didn't need the receptionist to be somebody's cousin. The woman on the other end of the line had a soft voice and didn't ask why. They never asked why.

She went on a Tuesday.

The clinic looked like a dentist's office on the inside. Beige walls. Magazines from 2019. A wall-mounted TV running HGTV with the sound off, a couple making faces at avocado-green countertops. Tasha sat in the corner with her hands folded in her lap and watched a woman across from her cry without making any sound, and she thought *that's gonna be me in an hour,* and she stood up and she walked out.

Made it three blocks before she had to sit down on a bus stop bench because her legs wouldn't hold her up.

She told herself it was the smell. The clinic smelled like rubbing alcohol and despair and she wasn't ready, that's all. She'd come back. She'd just needed to see the place first, see what she was walking into. She'd come back.

She booked another appointment. Wednesday. Different clinic, this one in Brooklyn, far from anybody who might know her face. She got as far as the parking lot. Sat in her car for forty minutes watching women go in and watching women come out, trying to remember why she was supposed to be one of them. She couldn't remember. So she drove home.

That night she stood naked in front of the bathroom mirror. Eight weeks, the doctor had said. Eight weeks meant nothing showed yet. Her stomach was flat. Her body was her own. There was nothing to prove this child existed except a paper test and a heartbeat she'd seen flicker on a screen at the first appointment, white and small as a firefly.

She put her hand on her stomach.

You shouldn't be here, she thought. *Your father is what he is. Your father has bodies on him. Your father is gonna die and break my heart twice—once when they bury him and once when I have to tell you who he was.*

But here was the thing she couldn't say out loud. The thing she hadn't told the woman on the phone, hadn't told the receptionist at either clinic, hadn't told the empty parking lot in Brooklyn:

She'd already loved this baby for two weeks.

Loved it the way you love something nobody else knows about yet. Loved it the way her mama must have loved her in 1989—sixteen and scared and stupid and pregnant and everybody saying don't keep it. Her mama had kept her. Worked two jobs. Cried in church. Made it work. Told Tasha the story a hundred times: *I was your age and I had nothing, and I kept you, and you was the best thing I ever did.*

Tasha was thirty-two. She had a salon job and an apartment and a savings account with $4,300 in it and a man who was gonna die.

But she had her mama's hips. Her mama's stubbornness. Her mama's track record.

She got dressed. Made tea. Did not call the clinic to reschedule.

In the morning she would tell D Roc she was getting rid of it.

She would lie because the truth was a thing that could be taken from her. The truth was a thing Carmen could use. The truth was a thing a bullet could end.

The truth would stay hers—in her body, in her hands—until the day it was too late for anybody to do anything about it.

She turned off the light.

CHAPTER FIFTEEN: THE HAITIAN

D Roc called Tasha seventeen times before she answered.

"Don't," she said. That was it. Just "don't."

"Is it true?"

"Would I lie about something like that?"

He was in the car still, parked on a side street in the Bronx, engine running, heat blasting even though he was sweating. His hands shook. Not from fear—he'd faced guns and didn't shake—but from something worse. Something that felt like his chest was caving in.

"How long you known?" he asked.

"Two weeks. Maybe three. I kept hoping I was wrong. Kept hoping my period was just late because of stress." Her voice cracked. "But I went to the clinic yesterday. They confirmed it. Eight weeks."

Eight weeks. D Roc did the math backwards. That put it at—fuck. Right before he killed Bishop. Right before everything went to shit. Back when they were still good. Back when she still looked at him like he was human.

"Tasha, I—"

"Don't say you're sorry. Don't say it's gonna be okay. Don't say none of that bullshit men say when they put a baby in someone and don't know what to do about it."

"What do you want me to say?"

"I want you to tell me the truth. Can you be a father? Can you keep this child safe? Can you—" She stopped, and he heard her crying. "Can you stop being what you are long enough to be what we need?"

D Roc closed his eyes. Saw the future like a movie he'd already watched. Saw Carmen's people coming for Tasha because he refused a job. Saw Rodrigo's crew taking his kid as collateral. Saw Detective Morrison using his child to pressure him into flipping. Saw a little boy or girl growing up with a father in prison or in the ground.

"I don't know," he said finally. "I'm in too deep. Got debts. Got enemies. Got cops building cases and cartels owning my ass. I don't know if I can keep anyone safe, including me."

"Then I already know my answer."

His heart stopped. "What answer?"

"I'm getting rid of it. Tomorrow. There's a clinic in Manhattan that—"

"No."

"Excuse me?"

"I said no. Don't do that. Please." D Roc didn't recognize his own voice. It sounded desperate. Broken. "I'll figure this out. I'll get clean. I'll—I'll find a way out of this shit. Just give me time."

"Time?" Tasha laughed, bitter and sharp. "You think time fixes this? You killed people, D. You work for a cartel. You got a million-dollar bounty on your head. Time don't fix none of that."

"I know, but—"

"And even if you survive—even if you somehow make it out alive—you think I want my child knowing what their father did? You think I want to explain why daddy's got bodies on his hands? Why people spit when they hear his name?"

"Our child," D Roc said quietly. "It's our child. Not just yours."

Silence. Long and heavy.

"I'm not keeping it," Tasha said finally. "I can't bring a baby into this hell you created. I won't."

"Tasha, please—"

"I'm done, D. Done with you. Done with this life. Done with hoping you'll change when we both know you can't." She was crying openly now. "I loved you. God, I loved you so much. But love don't pay bills and it don't stop bullets and it don't make dead people breathe again."

"Let me see you. One time. Face to face. Let me—"

"No. If I see you, I'll change my mind. And I can't afford to change my mind. Not about this." Her voice went hard. "Goodbye, D. I hope you find whatever you're looking for. I hope it was worth it."

She hung up.

D Roc sat there with a dead phone, feeling something inside him break that couldn't be fixed. Not with money. Not with violence. Not with anything.

He'd lost her. For real this time. And he'd lost a child he'd never meet.

Now he was nothing twice over.

He drove to a liquor store, bought a bottle of Hennessy with Carmen's money, and drank half of it in the parking lot. The burn felt good. Felt like punishment. Felt like what he deserved.

His phone buzzed. Not Tasha. Carmen.

Carmen: *Saturday is in 2 days. I need confirmation you're handling the Haitian.*

He typed back, fingers clumsy from the whiskey.

D Roc: *I'm on it.*

Carmen: *Good. Don't make me regret investing in you.*

Investing. Like he was stocks. Like he was property. Like he was anything other than a slave with a gun and a death wish.

He finished the bottle, threw it at a dumpster, missed. Then drove to Brooklyn to case the target.

The club was called Tropicana. Neon palm trees, bass thumping, line wrapped around the block even though it was Thursday night. Young kids waiting to get in, dressed like money they didn't have, hoping tonight was the night they became someone.

D Roc watched from across the street, smoking Newports, studying the security. Two big dudes at the door with earpieces. Cameras above the entrance. Probably more inside. The Haitian—Bertrand—was smart enough to invest in protection.

But smart wasn't the same as bulletproof.

D Roc had been doing this too long not to see the patterns. The shift change at 2 AM when the door guys rotated out. The side entrance by the kitchen where staff smoked between shifts. The windows on the second floor that didn't have bars.

He could get in. Kill Bertrand. Get out. Collect his fifty thousand and pay Rodrigo enough to buy another month of breathing room.

Simple. Clean. Easy.

Except it wasn't. Not anymore.

Every time he closed his eyes he saw Tasha crying. Saw the child that wouldn't exist because of him. Saw the future he'd murdered before it had a chance to breathe.

"Fuck," he whispered, crushing his cigarette under his Timbs.

A woman walked out of the club—early twenties, pretty, laughing with her friends. She looked happy. Looked like she didn't know the world was full of people like D Roc who turned everything they touched to ash.

He wondered if Bertrand had kids. Had a woman waiting at home. Had people who loved him and depended on him.

Then he remembered he didn't care.

Couldn't afford to care.

Caring is what got you killed.

By Friday afternoon, D Roc had a plan.

He'd go in through the kitchen entrance during the 2 AM shift change. Bertrand ran his office from the second floor—Carmen's folder had blueprints, guard rotations, everything. Two shots, center mass. One to the head to confirm. Then out the way he came.

No witnesses. No complications. Just work.

He was cleaning his .40—the same gun that killed Bishop, the same gun that fired on Trey—when his phone rang. Unknown number. He almost didn't answer.

"Yeah?"

"D Roc?" A kid's voice. Young. Scared.

"Who this?"

"Marcus. The kid you saved. Washington Heights."

D Roc sat up straight. The kid he'd spared. The one he gave money to run. "You okay? You get somewhere safe?"

"I tried. I really tried. But my grandma's sick and I couldn't just leave her and the money ran out and—" Marcus was crying now. "They found me. Carmen's people. They said I gotta work for them now. Said I owe them for letting me live."

D Roc's blood went cold. "Where are you?"

"I don't know. Some warehouse in Queens. They got me watching a stash house. Said if I don't do what they say, they'll kill my grandma. They'll kill her, Roc. They showed me pictures of her at church, at the grocery store, everywhere. They said—"

The line went dead.

D Roc tried calling back. Straight to voicemail.

He grabbed his jacket, his gun, his keys. Started for the door. Then stopped.

This was a trap. Had to be. Carmen testing him. Seeing if he'd run to save some kid instead of handling business. Seeing if he was loyal or if he was weak.

But what if it wasn't a trap? What if Marcus really was in trouble? What if Carmen really was that evil—using a sixteen-year-old kid as leverage?

Of course she was that evil. He'd seen what she did to Dre. To Tone. To everyone who crossed her.

D Roc stood there in the doorway, torn between two impossible choices.

Save the kid and betray Carmen. Or let the kid die and stay alive.

King or monster.

He chose monster.

He closed the door, sat back down, and finished cleaning his gun.

Because monsters don't save people. Monsters do their jobs.

And his job was killing the Haitian.

Saturday night came like a funeral procession.

D Roc showed up at Tropicana at 1:45 AM, dressed in all black, gun loaded, heart dead. He'd spent the past day and a half not thinking about Marcus. Not thinking about Tasha. Not thinking about Tone or Peezy or everyone he'd buried.

Just the job. Just the money. Just survival.

The kitchen entrance was exactly where Carmen's intel said it would be. Two workers smoking, laughing, not paying attention. He waited until they went back inside, then slipped in behind them.

The kitchen was hot, loud, smelling like jerk chicken and fryer oil. Cooks yelling in Creole, plates clanging, dishwasher running full blast. Nobody noticed one more person in black clothes.

He moved through the kitchen, through a hallway, up a set of back stairs. The music from downstairs vibrated through the walls—some dancehall track about money and women and living forever.

Second floor. Quieter up here. Office door at the end of the hall, light showing underneath.

D Roc pulled his gun, screwed on the suppressor he'd bought from one of Carmen's connects. Took a breath. Another. Then kicked the door open.

Bertrand was at his desk, counting money. Big dude, maybe six-three, gold chains, dreadlocks down his back. He looked up, saw the gun, and didn't even flinch.

"You're the one," Bertrand said in a thick Haitian accent. "Carmen's dog. I heard about you."

"Nothing personal," D Roc said.

"It's always personal." Bertrand leaned back in his chair, hands visible, not reaching for anything. "You know what's funny? I was about to make a deal with her. Was gonna back off her territory, pay tribute, do right. Was gonna call her tomorrow."

"Too late for that."

"Yeah. I figured." Bertrand smiled, sad and tired. "You got kids?"

D Roc didn't answer.

"I got three. Two boys, one girl. Baby girl just turned four last week. Wants to be a doctor." Bertrand's eyes went distant. "Their mama already knows what's coming. Told her last month if something happens to me, take the kids to Haiti. To family. Get them away from this life."

D Roc thought about Kenya. Tone's little sister. Thirteen years old, wants to be a doctor. The girl he'd borrowed half a million dollars to save. The reason Tone was dead.

Everybody's kids wanted to be doctors. Like that could save them from fathers like D Roc. Like that could wash the blood out of the money that paid for their books.

"Stop talking."

"Why? You gonna kill me either way. Might as well know who you're killing." Bertrand's smile faded. "I ain't a good man. Done bad things. Hurt people. Sold poison that destroyed families. But I loved my kids. That count for anything?"

"No," D Roc said.

He shot Bertrand twice in the chest. The suppressor made the shots sound like coughs. Bertrand slumped forward, blood spreading across his desk, soaking the money he'd been counting.

On the desk, half-hidden under papers, D Roc saw a photo. Three kids. Two boys, one girl. The four-year-old who wanted to be a doctor.

He didn't look away. Made himself see it. Made himself remember what he was taking from them.

D Roc walked closer, put one more in his head. Confirmation. Carmen wanted proof.

He pulled out his phone, took a picture. Sent it to Carmen with one word: *Done.*

Then he walked out the same way he came in. Through the hallway, down the stairs, through the kitchen. Nobody saw him. Nobody stopped him.

By 2:30 AM he was in his car, driving through Brooklyn, hands steady on the wheel, blood on his shoes.

His phone buzzed. Carmen.

Carmen: *Excellent. El Paraiso. Monday. Collect your payment.*

D Roc: *Send it.*

Carmen: *I prefer face to face. Monday. Noon. Don't make me ask again.*

He didn't respond. Just drove. Through Brooklyn, through Manhattan, across the bridge into Queens. Nowhere to go. Nowhere safe. Just moving because stopping meant thinking and thinking meant feeling and feeling meant remembering he'd just murdered a father because a Colombian woman told him to.

At a red light, he looked at himself in the rearview mirror.

Didn't recognize what he saw.

The eyes were wrong. Dead. The kind of dead that doesn't come back.

He'd finally become exactly what everyone said he was.

A monster who killed for money.

A slave who pretended to be a king.

Nothing wrapped in expensive clothes and cigarette smoke.

The light turned green.

He drove.

CHAPTER SIXTEEN: COLLATERAL

Rodrigo's people came for D Roc on Monday morning.

Not Carmen's people. Not cops. Not bounty hunters. Rodrigo's.

D Roc was in a diner in Queens—one of those 24-hour spots where nobody asks questions and the coffee tastes like cigarette ash—when two Dominicans in leather jackets walked in and sat on either side of him at the counter.

"Rodrigo wants his money," the one on the left said. Young dude, maybe twenty-five, scar across his eyebrow. "Today."

D Roc kept eating his eggs. "I got it. Tell him I'll bring it by Wednesday."

"He said today." The one on the right—older, gray in his beard—put his hand on D Roc's arm. Not aggressive. Just there. "He don't like waiting. Makes him nervous. And when Rodrigo gets nervous, people get hurt."

"I said Wednesday."

"And we said today." Scarface leaned closer. "You owe a million dollars. You been owing for three months now. Only payment you made was that fifty K two weeks ago. Rodrigo's getting impatient."

D Roc set down his fork, looked at both of them. "Y'all really wanna do this here? In public? With cameras and witnesses?"

Gray Beard smiled. "Cameras don't work in this place. Owner owes Rodrigo money too. And witnesses?" He looked around the empty diner—just them, one waitress reading a magazine, and a cook in the back. "I don't see no witnesses. Do you, hermano?"

"Nah," Scarface said. "I don't see shit."

D Roc's .40 was in his waistband, within reach. He could probably drop both of them before they pulled their own weapons. Probably. But then what? War with Rodrigo on top of everything else? Another crew trying to kill him?

"How much time I got?" he asked.

"Six PM. Washington Heights. Rodrigo's restaurant. You show up with fifty thousand or you don't show up at all." Gray Beard stood, dropped a twenty on the counter for D Roc's breakfast. "Consider this a professional courtesy. Next time we come, we ain't bringing money. We bringing body bags."

They left.

D Roc sat there, eggs getting cold, coffee getting colder, mind racing through math that didn't work.

He had twenty-five thousand from Carmen—half payment for the Bertrand hit. She owed him another twenty-five when he picked it up this afternoon. That was fifty total. Which covered Rodrigo's payment. Which left him at zero. Again.

And he still owed Rodrigo nine hundred and fifty thousand.

His phone buzzed. Detective Morrison.

"We need to talk," Morrison said.

"I told you—"

"I know what you told me. But things have changed. I got new information. Information that could put you away for life or set you free. Depends on what you do with it."

"I ain't interested."

"Even if I told you Carmen Vasquez is planning to kill you? That she's already put the order out? That you got maybe a week before her people come?"

D Roc went still. "You're lying."

"I'm not. We got a wire on one of her lieutenants. Heard the whole conversation. You're a liability now. You know too much, you're sloppy, and you're drawing heat. She's gonna tie up loose ends. You're the loosest end she's got."

"Why you telling me this?"

"Because I want her more than I want you. And my case is getting stronger every day—forensics, witnesses, security footage I'm piecing together. Help me build the rest and I'll put you in witness protection. New name, new city, new life. You'll be safe."

D Roc laughed. Bitter, broken. "Safe? Nigga, there ain't no safe. Carmen's got reach everywhere. Witness protection just means I die somewhere else."

"Then you're choosing to die here. In the next few days. Probably painfully." Morrison sighed. "Look, I've been chasing Carmen for five years. I'm close. I just need one witness. One person willing to testify about her operation. You do that, I can protect you. I promise."

"Your promises don't mean shit to me."

"Then what does? Because from where I'm sitting, you got nothing left to lose. Your crew's dead. Your woman's gone. You're broke, hunted, and working for people who plan to murder you. What exactly are you holding onto?"

D Roc didn't have an answer.

"Meet me," Morrison said. "Tomorrow. I'll show you what I have. Show you the wire recordings. Show you proof Carmen's coming for you. Then you decide. But at least see the evidence before you throw your life away."

"Where?"

"Riverside Park. Noon. Come alone. I come alone. Just two people talking."

"You're gonna arrest me."

"If I wanted to arrest you, I'd have done it already. I know where you sleep, where you eat, where you shit. I want Carmen. Help me get her and we both win."

Morrison hung up.

D Roc sat there, staring at his cold eggs, wondering if the detective was telling the truth or just running game. Wondering if Carmen really did plan to kill him or if this was Morrison trying to flip him with fear.

Either way, he was fucked.

He finished his coffee, left a tip, and walked out into cold November rain.

El Paraiso was empty when D Roc arrived at noon.

No hostess. No waiters. Just Carmen sitting at a table in the back, two bodyguards flanking her, and the smell of coffee and something cooking in the kitchen.

"Sit," she said.

D Roc sat.

Carmen pushed an envelope across the table. "Twenty-five thousand. As agreed. The Haitian's death was... efficient."

"That's what you pay for."

"Indeed." Carmen sipped her coffee, studied him over the rim. "You look tired."

"I am tired."

"Then rest. After the next job."

D Roc's jaw tightened. "There's always a next job with you, ain't it?"

"Of course. That's how employment works. I give you assignments. You complete them. I pay you. Simple arrangement."

"I want out."

Carmen's smile faded. "Excuse me?"

"I want out. Of this. Of working for you. I'll pay back whatever I owe, but I'm done killing for you."

"You don't owe me money. You owe me loyalty. There's a difference." Carmen set down her coffee. "And you don't get to quit. We've been over this."

"I'm not asking. I'm telling you. I'm done."

One of the bodyguards—the big one with the tombstone face—moved his hand to his waistband. D Roc caught the motion but didn't react.

Carmen held up a finger. The bodyguard stopped.

"You're upset," Carmen said calmly. "I understand. You've had losses. Your crew, your woman, your freedom. It's taking a toll. But quitting isn't an option. You know too much. You've done too much. Letting you walk away would be... problematic."

"So what, you kill me? Add another body to the pile?"

"If necessary." Carmen's voice was ice. "But I'd prefer not to. You're useful. Efficient. Discreet. I could train someone new, but that takes time. Easier to keep the tool I already have."

"I ain't your tool."

"You became my tool the moment you accepted my money. The moment you killed for me. You sold your soul, D Roc. Can't buy it back just because you got buyer's remorse."

D Roc stood up. "I'm leaving."

"Sit down."

"Fuck you."

The bodyguards moved. Fast. One grabbed D Roc's arm, the other pulled his gun. But D Roc was faster—he had his .40 out and pressed under Tombstone Face's chin before either of them could blink.

"I said I'm leaving," D Roc repeated. "Anybody moves, he dies first."

Carmen didn't flinch. "You really want to do this? Shoot my people? Start a war you can't win?"

"I'm already in a war I can't win. What's one more?"

They stood there, frozen. Mexican standoff in a Colombian restaurant. The absurdity wasn't lost on D Roc.

"Let him go," Carmen said finally.

The bodyguards released him but didn't lower their weapons.

D Roc backed toward the door, gun still aimed. "Stay away from me. Stay away from anyone I know. You come for me, I go to the cops. Tell them everything. Every name, every deal, every body. I'll burn your whole operation down."

"If you do that, you burn with it."

"I'm already burning." D Roc reached the door. "Maybe it's time I take some people with me."

He left.

Outside, the rain had stopped but the streets were wet. D Roc ran to his car, jumped in, and drove. Fast. Didn't know where he was going. Just away.

His phone buzzed before he hit the next block. Carmen.

Carmen: *You just made a very stupid decision. I gave you a chance to do this the easy way. Now we do it my way. You have 24 hours to reconsider. After that, everyone you've ever cared about becomes a target. Think carefully.*

D Roc threw the phone out the window. Watched it shatter on the asphalt in his rearview mirror.

He needed help. Needed allies. Needed something.

He called Dre. Straight to voicemail. Called three more times. Nothing.

Drove to Philadelphia. To the address where Dre was staying with Shanice.

The apartment building looked normal. No police tape. No signs of violence. He went to the fourth floor, knocked on the door.

Shanice answered. Her eyes were red from crying.

"Where's Dre?" D Roc asked.

"Gone."

"Gone where?"

"Gone gone. His mama's house got shot up last night. Twenty bullets through the front windows. His little sister was inside. She's okay but—" Shanice wiped her eyes. "Dre said he can't do this no more. Can't have his family dying because of your wars. He left. Said he's going somewhere you can't find him. Somewhere nobody can."

"Shanice, I—"

"Don't. Just don't." She started closing the door. "You're death, D Roc. Everybody around you dies or runs. I hope whatever you were fighting for was worth it."

The door closed.

D Roc stood there in the hallway, alone.

His last crew member was gone. His last friend had run. He was completely, totally alone.

He drove back to New York. Stopped at a bodega, bought a bottle of Hennessy and three packs of Newports. Sat in his car in a parking lot and drank and smoked until his lungs hurt and his head spun.

His burner phone buzzed—the one he kept for emergencies. Only three people had the number. Tone (dead), Dre (gone), and Nova.

Nova.

He answered. "Yeah?"

"I heard what happened." Nova's voice was quiet. Scared. "Heard Carmen put a price on your head. Heard Rodrigo's coming for you. Heard the cops are close. D, you need to disappear. Like really disappear. Get out of New York. Get out of the country if you can."

"I got nowhere to go."

"Then you're gonna die. You know that, right? There's no winning this. Too many people want you dead."

"I know."

"So why you still there? Why ain't you running?"

D Roc took a long pull from the bottle. "Because I'm tired of running. Tired of being scared. Tired of letting people control my life." He lit another Newport. "Maybe it's time I go down swinging. Take a few of them with me."

"That's suicide."

"Maybe. But at least I'll die on my feet."

"D, listen to me—"

"Nah. You listen. You got out. You made it. Don't look back. Don't try to save me. Just live your life and forget you ever knew me."

"I can't do that."

"You have to." D Roc's voice cracked. "I'm already dead, Nova. Been dead since I shook Carmen's hand. Since I killed Bishop. Since I chose this life over everything else. I'm just a ghost that don't know it yet."

"Then let me help you become something else. Let me—"

"Goodbye, Nova."

D Roc hung up. Turned off the phone. Threw it in the back seat.

He sat there drinking, smoking, watching normal people live normal lives. The kind of life he'd never have.

At 5:45 PM, he drove to Washington Heights. To Rodrigo's restaurant. With twenty-five thousand dollars—half of what he owed.

Better to face one enemy at a time.

Rodrigo was waiting in a booth in the back. Gray suit, silver watch, expensive cologne. He looked like a businessman. Which he was. The kind of businessman who broke legs when payments were late.

"You're short," Rodrigo said, counting the money.

"I know. It's half. I'll have the rest in two weeks."

"Two weeks." Rodrigo leaned back, fingers steepled. "You said that last time. And the time before. I'm starting to think you're stalling."

"I'm not. I just—shit's complicated right now."

"Complicated is your problem. My problem is I loaned you money and you're not paying it back." Rodrigo's eyes went hard. "I like you, D Roc. Always have. You're smart, you're resourceful, you don't panic. But business is business. And if I let you slide, everyone else gonna think they can slide too."

"What do you want?"

"I want my money. All of it. By the end of the month."

"That's three weeks. I can't—"

"Then I'll take it another way." Rodrigo pulled out a folder, slid it across. "Your territory. 118th Street. Sign it over to me. That clears the debt."

D Roc looked at the papers. A contract. Legal and binding. Giving away everything he'd built.

"That's my block."

"It WAS your block. Now it's collateral." Rodrigo lit a cigar, blew smoke at the ceiling. "You got two choices. Pay me nine hundred and fifty thousand by the end of the month, or sign that paper and walk away breathing. Those are your options."

"You know I can't pay that."

"Then sign."

D Roc stared at the contract. His kingdom on paper. His crown turned to words and signatures.

Everything he'd killed for. Everything he'd lost people for. Everything that made him King.

Gone.

"I need time to think," D Roc said.

"You got until Friday. After that, I start taking things by force. Your corners. Your connects. Your life. Choose wisely."

D Roc left without signing. Without agreeing. Without knowing what the fuck he was gonna do.

Outside, the city was dark and cold and full of people who wanted him dead.

He lit a Newport, felt the familiar burn, and laughed.

Because this was it. This was the endgame. Carmen wanted him dead. Rodrigo wanted his territory. Morrison wanted him to flip. Tasha wanted him gone. Dre was gone. Tone was dead. Peezy was dead.

And D Roc?

D Roc was standing on a corner in Washington Heights, smoking a cigarette, broke and hunted and alone.

But maybe—just maybe—he could be king one last time.

Not of territory or money or respect.

King of ashes.

King of blood.

King of the ruins he was about to create.

He pulled out his last phone—the one he hadn't thrown away yet—and made three calls.

First call: To Carmen's lieutenant. Left a message. "Tell Carmen if she wants me dead, come find me. I'll be on 118th Street. Friday night. Bring everyone."

Second call: To Rodrigo's second-in-command. Left a message. "Tell Rodrigo if he wants his money, come collect it. 118th Street. Friday night. I'll be waiting."

Third call: To Detective Morrison. Left a message. "You want Carmen? You want Rodrigo? They'll both be on 118th Street Friday night. Bring your whole department. Bring cameras. Bring everybody. I'm gonna give you the biggest bust of your career."

He hung up.

Threw the phone in a trash can.

Lit another Newport.

And smiled for the first time in weeks.

Because if he was going down, he wasn't going down alone.

He was taking everyone with him.

CHAPTER SEVENTEEN: THE LAST KINGDOM

Tuesday morning, D Roc went back to 118th Street for the first time in three weeks.

The crime scene tape was gone but the ghosts weren't. Yellow paint marked where Trey's boys had died. Bullet holes in brick. Blood stains the rain hadn't washed away. The block looked like a warzone that forgot to clean up.

A few old heads sat on stoops, smoking, watching him with eyes that had seen this story before. They knew what he was. Knew what was coming. Nobody said nothing. Just nodded once, slow, like they was acknowledging a funeral they'd already planned.

D Roc walked the block end to end. His kingdom. His territory. The place he'd killed for and buried friends for and lost his soul for.

It looked smaller than he remembered. Just a street. Just concrete and brick and trash cans. Nothing special. Nothing worth dying for.

But he'd die here anyway.

He lit a Newport, his first of the day but definitely not his last, and started making calls.

First call was to Manny at the strip club.

"Roc?" Manny sounded nervous. Always sounded nervous. "Man, I heard you got problems. Heard Carmen put a price on your—"

"I need weapons. Everything you got. ARs, AKs, shotguns, pistols, ammo. All of it."

"I can't. Carmen's people came by. Said anybody who helps you is dead. Said—"

"Manny. I'm already dead. Question is, you gonna help me go out with a bang or you gonna let Carmen own you forever?"

Silence.

"How much?" Manny asked finally.

"Whatever's fair. I got twenty-five thousand left."

"That ain't enough for what you asking."

"Then consider it a down payment. I die Friday, you keep the guns. I live, I pay you the rest."

"You ain't gonna live."

"I know. But the guns still got value, right? Sell them after. Make your money back and then some."

More silence. Then: "Noon. Behind the club. Cash only. And Roc? Don't come back after this. We ain't friends no more. Can't afford to be."

"We were never friends, Manny. Just business."

He hung up.

Second call was to a kid named Little Jay who ran numbers in the Bronx. Young dude, maybe nineteen, always hungry for a come-up.

"Yo, Roc! Man, I heard you was—"

"I need bodies. Friday night. 118th Street. There's gonna be a war and I need shooters."

"Against who?"

"Everyone. Carmen's crew, Rodrigo's people, maybe cops. It's gonna be ugly."

"Fuck you need me for then? Sounds like suicide."

"It is. But I'm paying five thousand a head. Show up with a gun and I'll pay you whether you live or die. Money goes to whoever you want—mama, girl, whoever. I'm dead anyway. Might as well spread the wealth."

"Five thousand just to show up?"

"And shoot. Gotta actually shoot. But yeah. Five K. Cash. Up front."

Little Jay whistled. "That's crazy money for a suicide mission."

"You in or out?"

"Let me talk to my boys. Call you back in an hour."

He hung up. D Roc knew the kid would probably take the money and run. Probably smart. But maybe—just maybe—some young hungry niggas would show up looking for glory and a payday.

Either way, D Roc would be alone when it mattered.

Always was.

By Tuesday afternoon, he had the weapons.

Manny delivered them in a van behind the strip club. Didn't say nothing, just unloaded crates and drove away fast, like D Roc's death was contagious.

The arsenal was impressive. Four AK-47s. Two AR-15s. Three shotguns. Six pistols. Enough ammo to fight a small army. Which is exactly what he'd be fighting.

D Roc loaded everything into his car and drove back to 118th Street. Found an abandoned building—one of the old brownstones that had been empty for years, squatters and junkies long since moved on—and carried everything inside.

Third floor. Apartment overlooking the street. Perfect vantage point.

He spent the rest of Tuesday and all of Wednesday fortifying. Moved furniture to create barriers. Taped magazines together for quick reloads. Positioned weapons at different windows. Planned sightlines and escape routes.

Not that he'd escape. But planning felt better than accepting.

Wednesday night, he went to see Tasha one last time.

He knew where she lived—same apartment in the projects on 121st. He knew the cops might be watching. Knew Carmen's people might be watching. Knew it was stupid.

Went anyway.

He stood outside her building in the rain, looking up at her window. Third floor. Lights on. She was home.

He pulled out his phone. Typed a message. Deleted it. Typed another. Deleted that too.

Finally just wrote: *I'm sorry. For everything. You deserved better than me. The baby deserved better than me. I hope you find it.*

He hit send. Watched the three dots appear, disappear, appear again.

Then her response: *I know.*

That was it. No "I love you." No "be safe." Just "I know."

D Roc stood there in the rain, staring at those two words, feeling something inside him crack that he didn't know was still whole.

He wanted to go up. Wanted to knock on her door. Wanted to hold her one more time and pretend they could fix this. Pretend they could run away together and start over somewhere clean.

But there was nowhere clean. Not for him. He'd tracked blood everywhere he went.

He turned and walked away. Didn't look back.

Some goodbyes don't need words.

Thursday morning, Little Jay called back.

"I got six shooters," he said. "They want ten K each, not five."

"Deal. But they show up ready. Body armor if they got it. Extra clips. And they stay till it's done. No running when shit gets hot."

"They know the deal. When you want them?"

"Friday. Eight PM. 118th Street. Third brownstone from the corner. Tell them to come through the back."

"Aight. But Roc? For real, you sure about this? This ain't regular beef. This is—"

"The end. Yeah. I know." D Roc lit a Newport, blew smoke at the ceiling. "That's exactly why I'm doing it."

Little Jay hung up.

D Roc sat there in the empty apartment, surrounded by guns, wondering if the six shooters would actually show. Wondering if it mattered.

He was one man. Maybe seven if the kids came through. Against Carmen's crew—at least twenty soldiers. Rodrigo's people—another fifteen. Cops who knew how many.

The math didn't work. Couldn't work. This wasn't about winning. This was about making sure everybody lost.

If he couldn't have his kingdom, nobody could.

Thursday afternoon, Detective Morrison called.

"You're making a mistake," Morrison said. "Whatever you're planning for tomorrow, don't."

"How you know I'm planning anything?"

"Because I know you. And I know when a man's given up on living and started planning his death. You called me to 118th Street tomorrow. You called Carmen and Rodrigo too. You're setting up a massacre."

"You don't know shit."

"I know you're gonna get people killed. Civilians. Bystanders. Kids who live on that block. Is that what you want? More bodies?"

D Roc didn't answer.

"Let me bring you in," Morrison said, softer now. "Protective custody. We do this the right way. I'll arrest you, sure, but you'll be alive. You'll have a chance to testify, to take down the people who destroyed your life. You'll have a future."

"I don't want a future. I want revenge."

"Revenge is just death with extra steps." Morrison sighed. "Look, I get it. You're angry. You lost people. You got backed into a corner. But this ain't the way out. This is just more blood. More mothers crying. More kids growing up without fathers. You really want that?"

"What I want don't matter no more. It's already in motion."

"Then stop it. Call it off. Walk away."

"Can't walk away from what I am. Can't wash off what I done." D Roc crushed his cigarette, lit another. "You want Carmen and Rodrigo? Be there tomorrow. Bring everybody. I'll gift wrap them for you. But I ain't going down quiet."

"D Roc—"

He hung up.

The rain started again. Always raining now. Like the city was crying for what was about to happen.

Thursday evening, D Roc took the A train to Woodlawn.

He hadn't been to see his mama in three years. Hadn't wanted to face her—or what was left of her—knowing what he'd become. But if tomorrow was the end, he owed her a goodbye.

Woodlawn Cemetery was quiet at dusk. Old trees. Rolling hills. Dead people who'd lived better lives than he ever would. His mama's grave was in the cheap section—a small headstone he'd paid for with drug money back when he still thought that meant something.

DENISE MARIE ROBINSON 1968-2015 Beloved Mother

D Roc stood there in the rain, Newport burning between his fingers, reading those words like they'd tell him something he didn't already know.

"Hey, Mama."

The wind rustled the trees. Somewhere a crow cawed.

"I know I ain't been around. I know you probably looking down at me and shaking your head. You always said the streets would swallow me. Said I was too smart for that life." He laughed, bitter. "Guess I wasn't as smart as you thought."

He crouched down, touched the wet grass in front of her headstone.

"I killed people, Mama. A lot of people. Some deserved it. Some didn't. I told myself it was survival. Told myself I didn't have a choice. But that's a lie, ain't it? There's always a choice. I just kept making the wrong one."

The rain picked up. D Roc didn't move.

"I got a son now. You'd have been a grandmother. His name is Marcus Tone—after people who died because of me. He'll never know me. That's probably for the best." His voice cracked. "Tasha's raising him right. She'll make sure he doesn't end up like his daddy."

He pulled out the .40, looked at it. The gun that started everything. The gun that would probably end it.

"Tomorrow I'm gonna do something stupid. Probably gonna die doing it. But I wanted to tell you—" He stopped. Swallowed hard. "I wanted to tell you

I'm sorry. For all of it. For not being the man you raised me to be. For letting you down. For becoming everything you warned me about."

He stood up, knees wet from the grass.

"If I see you tomorrow, I hope you ain't too disappointed. I hope you understand I tried. Even when I was doing wrong, I was trying to do right by my people. I just—" He wiped his eyes with his palm. "I just got lost somewhere. And now I can't find my way back."

He kissed his fingers, touched the headstone.

"I love you, Mama. Always did. Always will."

He walked away without looking back. Some conversations don't need a response. Some goodbyes are just for the person saying them.

The A train carried him back to Harlem, back to the block, back to the war waiting for him.

Thursday night, D Roc couldn't sleep.

He lay on the floor of the empty apartment, gun next to his head, staring at water stains on the ceiling. His mind wouldn't shut off.

Around 2 AM, he gave up trying. Got dressed, tucked his .40, and walked out into the night. Didn't know where he was going. Just needed to move.

He ended up at Rucker Park.

The courts were empty this late—chain-link fences locked, bleachers folded up, hoops standing silent against the orange city glow. D Roc stood at the fence, fingers hooked through the links, remembering.

He'd played here as a kid. Before the streets got him. Before the corners called his name. He'd been good, too—quick hands, decent jumper, the kind of player scouts came to watch in summer tournaments. His mama used to sit in those bleachers with her church friends, clapping every time he scored, screaming his real name like it meant something.

Darrell! That's my baby! Go, Darrell!

He couldn't remember the last time someone called him Darrell. Couldn't remember the last time he'd done anything that didn't involve guns or money or blood.

A car passed, bass thumping. The sound faded into the night.

D Roc stood there for an hour, just watching the empty court. Remembering who he used to be before he became who he was. The kid who loved basketball. Who had a mama who loved him. Who thought he might make it out someday.

That kid was dead. Had been dead for years.

But standing here, in the quiet before the storm, D Roc mourned him anyway.

"Sorry, little man," he whispered to the ghost of himself. "I tried."

He walked back to the apartment as the first gray light crept over the East River.

There, he lay on the floor, gun next to his head, staring at water stains on the ceiling. His mind still wouldn't shut off.

Saw Peezy's face. Saw Tone's eyes. Saw Marcus burning. Saw Lil Marcus dying in his arms. Saw Bishop's brains on the barbershop floor. Saw Trey bleeding in Newark. Saw Bertrand slumped over his money.

Saw Tasha crying. Saw the baby she was carrying—the one he'd never hold. Saw his mama's grave—dead ten years now, cancer taking her slow. Wondered what she'd think of what he'd become.

She'd probably cry. Or maybe she already knew. Maybe the dead always knew.

He got up, paced the room, smoked until his lungs burned and his throat was raw. Checked the weapons for the hundredth time. Made sure everything was loaded, ready, positioned right.

The block outside was quiet. 3 AM quiet. Nothing moving except cats and rats and the occasional car with somewhere better to be.

D Roc looked out the window at his kingdom.

118th Street. His block. His territory. The place that made him King.

Tomorrow it would burn. Tomorrow it would run red with blood. Tomorrow it would become something out of a nightmare.

And D Roc would be at the center of it, conducting the violence like a symphony he'd been writing since the first time he picked up a gun.

But for one night—one last night—he was still King of something.

Friday arrived like a death sentence.

D Roc woke at dawn, if you could call it waking when he never really slept. The sun came up blood-red, dyeing the East River the color of everything D Roc had spilled.

He showered in cold water—the building's heat didn't work—and put on fresh clothes. Black jeans. Black hoodie. Black Timbs. War colors.

Strapped his .40 to his hip. The same gun that started all of this. The same gun that would end it.

He made coffee on a camp stove he'd stolen from somewhere. Drank it black and bitter. Smoked five Newports before noon.

Then he went to visit his crew.

First stop was the spot where Peezy died. Someone had left flowers—probably his mama—but they were dead now, brown and wilted. D Roc added a Newport to the pile, unlit. Tribute.

"I'm sorry, young blood," he said to the empty street. "I'm sorry I got you killed. I'm sorry I wasn't better. But I'ma make it right. Tonight, everybody who contributed to your death—they gonna pay. I promise."

The wind blew. Silence answered.

Second stop was the basketball court where Tone died. The blood was gone but D Roc still saw it. Saw Tone's eyes. Saw the knife pinned to his chest.

"You were right," D Roc said, lighting a cigarette and leaving it burning on the concrete. "About all of it. We were dead men walking. I just didn't wanna see it. But I see it now, bro. I see it clear. And tonight, I'ma finish what we started. I'ma be the king you thought I was. Even if it's only for an hour."

A kid rolled past on a bike, stared at D Roc talking to nothing, kept moving.

Third stop was Marcus's mama's house. He didn't go inside. Just stood across the street, looking at the windows, remembering a sixteen-year-old kid who wanted to help his mama and got burned alive for it.

"I failed you," D Roc whispered. "Failed you and every kid who looked up to me and thought I was somebody worth following. But maybe—maybe if I take enough of them with me—maybe that counts for something. Maybe that makes it mean something."

It didn't. He knew it didn't. But he said it anyway.

By 6 PM, the sun was setting and D Roc was back in the apartment.

Little Jay's six shooters showed up at 7. Young kids, nineteen to twenty-two, looking scared and excited and hungry. D Roc paid them each ten thousand cash. Half of them probably wouldn't make it to midnight.

"Rules are simple," D Roc said, showing them the weapons. "Don't shoot unless you see a gun. Don't shoot cops unless they shoot first. Anybody in body armor, aim for the legs or head. And if shit gets too hot, you can bounce. I ain't gonna judge. This is my war, not yours. You just here for the paycheck."

"Who we fighting?" one kid asked. Baby face, couldn't have been twenty.

"Everybody." D Roc lit a Newport. "Colombian cartel. Dominican crew. Maybe police. Maybe more. I called them all here. They all want me dead. So we gonna make them work for it."

"That's crazy."

"Yeah. It is." D Roc smiled, cold and mean. "That's why I'm paying so much. Y'all ready?"

They nodded, but their eyes said they weren't. Nobody was ready for what was coming.

At 7:30, the first crew arrived.

Black SUVs. Four of them. Carmen's people. They parked at the end of the block and started setting up. D Roc watched through binoculars. Counted fifteen men. All armed. All wearing body armor.

Professional. Organized. Ready to end this.

At 7:45, Rodrigo's crew showed up.

Different vehicles. Mix of cars and trucks. Maybe twelve men. Less organized than Carmen's but just as dangerous. They took positions on the opposite end of the block, eyeing Carmen's crew with suspicion.

Nobody was sure who was the enemy yet.

At 8:00, the cops arrived.

Unmarked cars. Plain clothes. But D Roc recognized Morrison's sedan. The detective parked two blocks away, probably thinking D Roc wouldn't notice. But D Roc noticed everything tonight.

His last night. His last stand. His last chance to mean something.

At 8:15, the block was surrounded.

Carmen's crew on the east. Rodrigo's crew on the west. Cops setting up a perimeter. And D Roc in the middle, three floors up, with six kids who didn't know what they'd signed up for and enough weapons to start a small war.

"Here we go," D Roc said to nobody. To everybody. To the ghosts of everyone he'd killed and everyone who'd died for him.

He lit one more Newport. Chain-smoked half of it. Felt the nicotine burn. Felt the familiar calm of knowing death was seconds away.

Then he picked up the AK-47, walked to the window, and fired three shots into the air.

The signal.

The declaration.

The beginning of the end.

For a half-second, the block was silent. Confused. Everyone looking around, trying to figure out where the shots came from.

Then all hell broke loose.

Carmen's crew opened fire on Rodrigo's crew. Rodrigo's crew fired back. Cops started yelling through megaphones. Civilians ran screaming. Windows shattered. Cars exploded.

And D Roc stood in the window, AK-47 spraying bullets, laughing like a man who'd finally accepted what he was.

A monster.

A king.

A ghost dancing in the ruins of his own kingdom.

The war for 118th Street had begun.

CHAPTER EIGHTEEN: ARMAGEDDON

The first casualty was a kid named Malik.

He was at the window when Carmen's crew figured out where the shots came from. Return fire lit up the third floor like lightning. Malik took three rounds to the chest before he could duck. Body armor caught two. The third went through his neck.

He dropped, gurgling, hands clutching at nothing.

"Fuck! FUCK!" Baby Face—the twenty-year-old—scrambled away from the window, eyes wide with terror. "They killing us!"

"That's the point!" D Roc returned fire, AK-47 spitting lead. Dropped one of Carmen's soldiers in the street. The man went down screaming, leg shattered. His partners dragged him behind an SUV.

"Get on a different window!" D Roc shouted. "Spread out! Don't bunch up!"

Baby Face moved to another window, hands shaking so bad he could barely hold his gun. D Roc caught a glimpse of his face—tears streaming, but still fighting. Still there.

"Why you here?" D Roc asked between shots. "You could've run with the money."

"My little brother," Baby Face said, firing wild at the street below. "He's twelve. Looks up to me. I can't—" he ducked as return fire shattered the window frame, "—I can't let him see me be a coward. Rather he find out I died fighting than ran like a bitch."

"He'd rather have a live coward than a dead hero."

"Nah." Baby Face's jaw set, suddenly looking older than twenty. "He wouldn't. Not in our world."

The kids scrambled. Some listened. Some froze. This was their first real gunfight. Probably their last.

Down on the street, Rodrigo's crew and Carmen's crew had figured out they had a common enemy. Both started advancing on D Roc's building, using cars as cover, coordinated fire keeping D Roc's shooters pinned.

D Roc switched to the AR-15. Better accuracy. Aimed for a Dominican in a leather jacket. Squeezed twice. Both shots hit center mass. The man fell backwards, dead before he touched pavement.

"They're coming up the stairs!" Little Jay yelled from the hallway. "I hear them!"

"Block the door! Use the furniture!" D Roc didn't turn around, kept firing. Another target. Another squeeze. Another body. The math was simple. Kill faster than they could advance.

But there were too many. Always too many.

Glass exploded behind him. Bullets tore through the apartment. One of the kids—a skinny dude with braids—caught a round in the shoulder, spun, went down. Not dead but screaming. Bleeding bad.

"Help him!" D Roc snapped at Baby Face.

"With what?! I'm not a fucking doctor!"

"Then make him shut up! His screaming's gonna draw more fire!"

Baby Face crawled to Braids, tried to stop the bleeding with his hands. Blood everywhere. Too much blood.

D Roc lit a Newport between shots. Hands steady. Muscle memory. He'd become the thing he always pretended to be. A machine. A weapon. Death in human form.

Down below, the cops were trying to establish a perimeter but the crossfire was too heavy. Morrison's voice came through a megaphone: "CEASE FIRE! NYPD! EVERYONE DROP YOUR WEAPONS!"

Nobody listened. Carmen's crew lit up a cop car. Rodrigo's people fired on Carmen's. D Roc fired on everybody.

The block was a killzone. Hell with streetlights.

At 8:47 PM, Carmen's crew breached the ground floor.

D Roc heard the explosion—they'd blown the door with something heavy—then boots pounding stairs. Fast. Disciplined. Professional.

"They're coming through!" Little Jay posted up at the apartment door with a shotgun, hands shaking. "What do we do?"

"We hold." D Roc ejected an empty mag, slapped in a fresh one. "They gotta come through that door. Make every inch cost them blood."

The first man up the stairs got his head blown off. Little Jay's shotgun did its job. Point-blank range. No mercy. The body tumbled backwards, taking two more men down with it.

But more came. Always more.

Bullets punched through the door. Little Jay dove left. Wasn't fast enough. Took one in the leg, went down screaming.

D Roc grabbed the other AR, sprayed the doorway blind. Heard someone yell in pain. Bought them seconds.

"Fall back!" D Roc pulled Little Jay deeper into the apartment. The kid was crying, clutching his leg, blood pumping between his fingers.

"I'm hit! I'm fucking hit!"

"You ain't dead. Stop crying and shoot." D Roc shoved a pistol in his hand. "Anybody comes through that door, empty the clip."

Baby Face and two others were still at windows, trading fire with the crews below. Braids was unconscious, maybe dead. Malik definitely dead. That left four shooters still in the fight.

Four against twenty. Maybe twenty-five now. The math kept getting worse.

The door exploded inward. Breaching charge. Four men rushed in—Carmen's crew, all tactical gear and dead eyes.

D Roc dropped the first with the AK. Little Jay got the second with wild pistol fire. The other two took cover behind overturned furniture, started suppressing fire.

Baby Face turned from his window, tried to line up a shot. Took a three-round burst to the face. His head snapped back. He collapsed without a sound.

D Roc saw him fall. Thought about a twelve-year-old boy who'd never know his brother died trying to be brave for him. Another kid who'd grow up with a ghost instead of family.

"NO!" one of the other kids screamed. Started spraying blind, panicked. Got lit up by return fire. Chest, stomach, arms. He danced like a puppet on strings then fell.

Two shooters left. D Roc and Little Jay.

Against everyone.

D Roc threw a grenade—one of the few he had left. It rolled behind the furniture where Carmen's men hid. They saw it, tried to run. Too late. The explosion blew them apart, blew out windows, set fire to curtains.

The apartment was burning now. Smoke filling the space. Harder to breathe. Harder to see.

"We gotta move!" Little Jay limped toward the back window. "We stay here, we cook!"

"Then jump. I'm staying."

"You're fucking crazy!"

"Yeah." D Roc reloaded, walked back to the front window. "Always have been."

Little Jay stared at him for a second. Then climbed out the window onto the fire escape. D Roc heard him clanging down metal stairs. Heard him hit the ground. Heard gunfire. Heard him scream.

Then silence.

D Roc was alone.

He lit another Newport. The pack was almost empty. Didn't matter. Wouldn't need them much longer.

The apartment was an inferno behind him. Smoke so thick he could barely see. But the window facing the street was clear enough.

Clear enough to aim.

He picked up the last AK, checked the mag. Half full. Good enough.

Down below, both crews were still fighting each other AND trying to breach his building. Rodrigo's people on one side, Carmen's on the other, cops trying to push in from the north.

Complete chaos. Beautiful chaos.

Through the smoke, D Roc caught a glimpse of Carmen herself—behind her SUV, firing a small silver pistol at Rodrigo's men who'd gotten too close. The Colombian queen getting her hands dirty. He'd never seen her shoot before. She was good. Calm. Every shot deliberate. Three of Rodrigo's soldiers dropped before they even knew she was armed.

D Roc aimed at a Dominican with a shotgun. Fired. Missed. Fired again. Hit him in the back. The man went down.

Aimed at one of Carmen's lieutenants—the big one with the tombstone face. Fired three times. Body armor caught two. Third caught his knee. He collapsed, roaring in pain.

Aimed at a cop car. Emptied the rest of the mag into it. Windows shattered, tires popped, but the cops inside survived. Scrambled out, took cover.

Morrison was down there somewhere. Probably regretting believing D Roc's call. Probably wishing he'd brought SWAT. Brought the army. Brought God himself.

D Roc dropped the empty AK, picked up an AR. Last rifle. After this, just pistols. After pistols, just hands. After hands, just dying.

But he wore it anyway.

At 9:15 PM, the building started collapsing.

The fire had spread. Support beams weakening. The whole structure groaning like a dying beast.

D Roc felt the floor shift under his feet. Heard cracking sounds. Knew he had minutes.

Good. Dying in a fire was poetic. Everything he'd burned—Marcus's body, Bishop's money house, the Newark penthouse—coming back to claim him.

He fired out the window. Dropped two more targets. Couldn't tell who they belonged to anymore. Everybody looked the same through smoke and blood and rage.

His phone buzzed. The burner. He'd forgotten he still had it.

Tasha.

He almost didn't answer. What was there to say?

"Yeah?"

"I'm watching the news." Her voice was shaking. "They're showing 118th Street. They're saying there's a massacre. Saying dozens dead. Saying—" She stopped. "Is that you? Are you there?"

"Yeah."

"D, what did you do?"

"What I had to." D Roc fired three more shots. Heard someone scream. "What I was always gonna do."

"You're gonna die."

"I know."

"Was it worth it? All of this? All the bodies? All the blood? Was any of it worth it?"

D Roc looked around the burning apartment. At the bodies of kids he'd paid to die. At the block below tearing itself apart. At his kingdom burning to ash.

"No," he said quietly. "None of it was."

"Then why?"

"Because I didn't know how to be nothing else." He crushed his cigarette on the windowsill. "I'm sorry, Tasha. For everything. For the baby. For making you love a monster. For—"

The floor gave out beneath him.

He dropped through to the second floor, landing hard, phone flying from his hand. Pain exploded through his ribs. Couldn't tell if they were broken or bruised or just screaming.

He rolled, coughing, smoke everywhere. Found an AR, grabbed it. Checked himself—nothing critical hit. Just hurt. Everything hurt.

Above him, the third floor collapsed completely. Burning debris falling like rain.

He stumbled to a window. Second floor now. Closer to the street. Closer to everyone trying to kill him.

Fine. Let them come.

He smashed out the window with the rifle butt, took position, started firing.

At 9:33 PM, Rodrigo's crew breached the second floor.

D Roc heard them coming. Three men. Maybe four. Heavy boots. Tactical movement.

He didn't wait. Grabbed the last grenade, pulled the pin, threw it down the hallway.

"GRENADE!"

The explosion was massive. Blew out walls. Brought down more ceiling. The screaming that followed told him he'd hit at least one.

But more kept coming. Always more.

D Roc fell back to the corner room. Last stand. Only one entrance. Good defensive position.

He had one AR with half a mag. Two pistols. His .40 and a backup Glock he'd taken from one of the dead kids. Maybe sixty rounds total.

Not enough. Never enough.

But enough to make them remember him.

The first man through the door took four rounds to the chest. Dropped. The second was faster, got behind cover, returned fire. D Roc felt something hot slice his left arm. Grazed. Not serious.

He fired blind around the corner. Heard cursing in Spanish. Hit something.

Silence.

Waiting.

D Roc's breathing was harsh, labored. Smoke inhalation. Blood loss. Exhaustion. His body was shutting down but his mind was crystal clear.

This was it. This was the end. And somehow, impossibly, he was okay with it.

He'd been dead for weeks. Months. Maybe years. Just took this long to make it official.

"D Roc!" A voice from the hallway. Rodrigo himself. "You're surrounded! Give up! Maybe I let you live!"

D Roc laughed. Bitter, broken. "You don't let nobody live! And I sure as shit ain't surrendering!"

"Then you die!"

"I've been dying! This is just catching up!"

More gunfire. D Roc returned it. The AR clicked empty. He dropped it, pulled both pistols. John Woo shit. Stupid but satisfying.

He stepped into the hallway, both guns blazing.

Dropped one man. Clipped another. Took return fire—one round hit his vest, felt like a hammer to the chest. Another grazed his thigh. He kept firing. Kept moving. Kept killing.

Until both pistols clicked empty.

He stood there in the burning hallway, guns empty, body broken, surrounded by the dead and dying.

And smiled.

"That all you got?" he yelled to whoever was left. "That's it? That's the best you got?"

Rodrigo stepped into the hallway. He'd lost his suit jacket. His white shirt was splattered with blood—his or someone else's. He had a gun but didn't raise it.

"You destroyed everything," Rodrigo said. "Killed my people. Burned your block. For what? For pride?"

"For principle," D Roc said. "I ain't nobody's slave. Not yours. Not Carmen's. Not nobody's. I'd rather die free than live on my knees."

"Then you're a fool."

"Maybe." D Roc swayed, legs barely holding him. "But I'm a fool who made y'all work for it."

Rodrigo raised his gun.

Then the wall exploded.

Not from grenades. From gunfire. From outside. Carmen's crew firing rocket launchers—actual fucking rocket launchers—into the building.

The explosion threw D Roc backwards. Threw Rodrigo sideways. The building shook like an earthquake. More of the second floor collapsed.

D Roc crawled through debris, ears ringing, vision blurred. Found his .40—his original gun, the one that started everything. Still had one mag left. His last mag.

He loaded it with shaking hands. Stood up. Barely.

Through the smoke, he saw Rodrigo.

The Dominican kingpin was pinned under a collapsed beam, half his body crushed, blood pooling black in the dim light. His silver watch still gleamed. His expensive suit was ruined. In his hand, clutched like a talisman, was a wallet—fallen open to show a photo. Three girls. Quinceañera dresses. Graduation caps.

He was still alive. Barely.

Their eyes met.

"My girls..." Rodrigo whispered, blood bubbling on his lips. "They won't know... what happened to me... they'll think..."

"They'll think you died a businessman," D Roc said. "They don't need to know nothing else."

"The debt..." Rodrigo coughed blood. "It dies with me..."

D Roc stood over the man who'd owned him. The man who'd loaned him a million dollars. The man who'd helped create this hell. The man who'd shown him pictures of his daughters and said *innocent don't mean much in our world.*

"Yeah," D Roc said. "It does."

Rodrigo's hand tightened on the wallet. "Tell them... tell them their father loved them..."

"I ain't telling them nothing. But they knew. They always knew."

Rodrigo tried to laugh but only blood came out. "King of Nothing... that's what you are... you got your... freedom..."

He died with his eyes on the photo. Not on D Roc. Not on the ceiling. On his daughters' faces. The last thing he saw was something good.

D Roc felt something crack in his chest. Not grief—he'd killed too many to grieve for one more. But recognition. Rodrigo wasn't so different from him. Just a man trying to keep the people he loved safe from the life he'd chosen. And failing. Like they all failed. Like D Roc had failed.

The building was coming down. Burning and collapsing and dying just like him.

Time to go.

He stumbled toward the stairs. Down. Had to get down. Had to get to the street. Had to finish this face to face.

First floor. Front door. Or what was left of it.

He kicked through debris, stepped outside.

The block was hell.

Cars burning. Bodies everywhere. Blood running in gutters. Buildings on fire. Civilians crying, hiding, dying. Cops trying to evacuate people while dodging bullets.

And in the middle of it all, Carmen.

She stood next to a black SUV, watching the chaos like a queen surveying her kingdom. Four bodyguards around her. All armed. All ready.

She saw D Roc. Smiled.

"There he is," she said. "The man who destroyed everything. Was it worth it?"

D Roc raised his .40. Hands shaking. Vision swimming. "You tell me."

Carmen's smile faded. "Kill him."

Her bodyguards raised their weapons.

D Roc fired first.

CHAPTER NINETEEN: KING OF ASHES

D Roc's first shot hit the bodyguard on the left. Neck shot. The man went down choking on his own blood.

The other three opened fire.

D Roc dove behind a burned-out car. Bullets sparked off metal. He rolled, came up firing. Two shots. One hit body armor. The other caught a bodyguard in the face. He dropped like someone cut his strings.

Two bodyguards left. Plus Carmen.

D Roc's .40 had maybe six rounds remaining. His last six rounds. After that, he was done.

The bodyguards were flanking him. One went left, one went right. Professional. Coordinated. They'd done this before.

But D Roc had been doing this longer.

He waited. Let them think they had him pinned. Let them get confident. Then he moved—not backward like they expected, but forward. Straight at the one on the left.

The bodyguard wasn't ready. D Roc was inside his guard before he could adjust. Point-blank range. Three shots to the chest. The vest caught two. The third went through his armpit where the vest didn't cover. The man screamed, fell.

The last bodyguard had a clear shot now. Fired. Hit D Roc's vest. Another hammer blow. D Roc staggered but stayed up. Turned. Fired his last two rounds.

Both hit. One in the throat. One in the face.

The bodyguard went down.

D Roc's .40 clicked empty. He dropped it. His original gun. The gun that started everything. Empty now. Done.

Just like him.

Carmen stood there, alone, watching him. She had a gun in her hand—a small silver pistol, elegant like everything else about her. The slide was locked back. Empty. She'd been firing during the chaos, D Roc realized. Protecting herself when her bodyguards couldn't. Even queens got their hands dirty when it mattered.

"Well," she said calmly, looking at the empty gun, then back at him. "Here we are."

"Here we are." D Roc's voice was ragged. He could barely stand. Broken ribs. Gunshot wounds. Blood loss. Running on nothing but spite and stubbornness.

"You destroyed everything," Carmen said. "My operation. My people. Years of work. For what? Pride?"

"Freedom." D Roc took a step toward her. Then another. "I ain't nobody's slave."

"You were never a slave. You were an employee. There's a difference."

"Not to me."

Carmen dropped the empty pistol. It clattered on the pavement. She didn't run. Didn't beg. Just stood there, watching him approach with those cold eyes that had seen a hundred men die.

"I was sixteen when I killed my first man," she said quietly. "I always knew I'd die the same way I lived. Violently. By someone hungrier than me." She almost smiled. "I just didn't think it would be some corner boy from Harlem."

"I ain't a corner boy no more."

"No. You're not." She straightened her jacket, smoothed her hair. Facing death like she was facing a business meeting. "Do it then. But know this—you didn't win. You just survived longer. That's not the same thing."

D Roc picked up a pistol from one of her dead bodyguards. Aimed at Carmen.

She didn't beg. Didn't plead. Just stood there, elegant even in defeat. "You think killing me ends this? My organization is bigger than one person. They'll send someone else. Someone worse."

"Let them." D Roc's hand was steady now. "I'll kill them too."

"You'll die first. If not from my people, then from the cops. From Rodrigo's crew. From cancer or old age or just bad luck. You can't win, D Roc. Nobody wins this game."

"I know." D Roc pulled the trigger.

Carmen fell. Clean shot. Center mass. She hit the ground and didn't move.

The Colombian queen was dead.

D Roc stood there for a moment, looking at her body. Felt nothing. No satisfaction. No relief. Just empty.

He dropped the gun. Turned to walk away.

"D Roc!" A voice from behind. "NYPD! Hands up!"

Detective Morrison. Standing thirty feet away with his service weapon drawn. Behind him, a dozen cops moving in, trying to secure the scene.

D Roc didn't put his hands up. Just stood there, swaying, bleeding, barely conscious.

"It's over," Morrison said. "You're under arrest."

"For what? Self-defense? They shot first. All of them." D Roc gestured at the carnage. "You got cameras everywhere. You got witnesses. They came here to kill me. I just killed them first."

"You started this war!"

"No. Bishop started it. Trey escalated it. Carmen made it worse. I just finished it." D Roc lit a cigarette—found a crushed pack of Newports in his pocket, one left. Miracle. "And now it's done."

"You killed thirty people!"

"They killed my crew first. Peezy. Tone. Marcus. How many bodies they get before I'm allowed to fight back?"

Morrison's jaw was tight. His gun didn't waver. But he didn't move closer either. "You can't just walk away from this."

"Watch me."

More cops were arriving. SWAT. ESU. The entire NYPD converging on 118th Street. But in the chaos—the fires, the bodies, the civilians running and screaming—nobody had a clear shot. Nobody knew who was who. Nobody could make sense of the massacre.

D Roc started walking. Slowly. Deliberately. Down the block. His block. Through the wreckage of his kingdom.

"Stop!" Morrison yelled. "I will shoot you!"

D Roc kept walking. Didn't look back. Didn't care.

Morrison didn't shoot. Maybe he couldn't. Maybe he didn't want to add another body to the count. Maybe he knew D Roc was already a dead man walking.

D Roc reached the end of the block. Turned the corner. Disappeared into the darkness.

Behind him, 118th Street burned.

He walked for hours. Through Harlem. Through the Bronx. Nowhere specific. Just walking. Bleeding. Dying slowly.

His phone buzzed. Somehow it still worked. Tasha.

He answered. "Yeah?"

"I saw it on the news." Her voice was shaking. "They're saying thirty-seven dead. They're saying it's the worst gang violence in city history. They're saying—" She stopped. "Are you alive?"

"Barely."

"D, you need a hospital. You're hurt. I can hear it."

"I'm fine."

"You're not fine! You're never fine! You're—" She was crying now. "Why? Why did you do this?"

"I told you. I had to."

"You didn't have to! You could have run! Could have left! Could have chosen anything else!"

"And then what? Live my whole life looking over my shoulder? Waiting for Carmen to send somebody? Waiting for Rodrigo to collect? That ain't living. That's just slow dying."

"So you chose fast dying instead?"

"I chose freedom." D Roc stopped walking, leaned against a wall. Everything hurt. "Even if it kills me."

"It already did." Tasha's voice went soft. "The D I loved died a long time ago. This is just his ghost finishing business."

"Maybe."

"I didn't do it." She said it flat. Matter-of-fact.

D Roc's world tilted. "What?"

"The clinic. I went twice. Couldn't go through with it." She laughed bitterly. "Maybe I'm stupid. Maybe I'm gonna regret it. Maybe I'm just selfish and don't wanna be alone in this. But I'm keeping our baby."

"Tasha—"

"I shouldn't. I know. I should save this child from having your blood. From growing up with the kind of stories people tell about you. But I can't get rid of it. I tried. God knows I tried."

"That's... that's good. That's—" D Roc didn't know what it was. His mind couldn't process. A child. His child. Growing inside Tasha while the world burned down around them.

"Don't come looking for us," Tasha said. "Don't try to be a father. Don't try to be anything. Just... disappear. Die. Let us pretend you never existed."

"I can't—"

"Yes you can. It's the only decent thing you got left to do. Die quietly and let us live." She paused. "Goodbye, D."

She hung up.

D Roc stood there in the dark, holding a dead phone, feeling whatever was left of his heart crack completely.

He had a child coming. A son or daughter. A piece of him that would survive even after he was gone.

And he'd never meet them. Never hold them. Never tell them he loved them.

Because Tasha was right. The best thing he could do was disappear. Be a ghost. A cautionary tale. A name the kid would hear whispered when people talked about the bad old days.

Father of nothing.

Nothing all the way down.

He made it back to 118th Street as the sun came up.

The block was destroyed. Worse than he'd imagined. Buildings burned to foundations. Cars overturned and charred. Blood everywhere. Bodies covered with sheets.

Crime scene tape wrapped around everything. Cops and forensics teams picking through the wreckage. News vans lined up, reporters doing live shots with the devastation as backdrop.

D Roc watched from a distance. Hidden in shadow. Seeing what he'd created.

A graveyard. A warzone. A monument to violence.

His kingdom.

He saw Detective Morrison talking to the press. Saw him explain that the violence was gang-related. Cartel conflict. That the NYPD was investigating. That arrests would be made.

But D Roc knew better. They had no witnesses. Everyone was dead or scattered. The security cameras were destroyed. The evidence was literal ashes.

They couldn't prove he started it. Couldn't prove anything except that a lot of people killed each other and the block burned.

Carmen was dead. Her organization would collapse without her. Rodrigo was dead—D Roc had seen his body in the rubble. The Dominicans would fight each other for what was left. The cops would chase shadows.

And D Roc?

D Roc had won.

He'd killed everyone who wanted him dead. Destroyed everyone who tried to own him. Stood alone at the end when everyone else fell.

He'd won the war.

But what did he win?

He looked at 118th Street. His territory. His block. His kingdom.

Nothing but ashes and ghosts.

No crew. No connect. No future. Just ruins and the memory of everyone he'd killed to get here.

The crown had finally fallen, and there was nothing left to rule.

Over the next few weeks, D Roc watched from the shadows as the block tried to rebuild.

The city cleared the bodies. Tore down the unstable buildings. Sent in crews to clean up the mess. Within a month, 118th Street looked almost normal. If you didn't know, you'd never guess dozens of people died there.

But D Roc knew. He'd see it forever.

The Colombians sent people to investigate Carmen's death. They sniffed around. Asked questions. But with no body to question and no witnesses to flip, they eventually gave up. Wrote off the New York operation as a loss. Moved on to other cities.

Rodrigo's people fought each other for weeks. Shootings every night in Washington Heights. Eventually, someone emerged on top—D Roc didn't care who. That wasn't his problem anymore.

The cops never found him. Morrison put out a warrant but without evidence, it was just paper. D Roc stayed hidden. Moved every few days. Different boroughs. Different faces. Became a ghost in his own city.

His wounds healed. Slowly. He found a veterinarian who patched him up for cash, no questions asked. The ribs took longest. Still hurt when he breathed deep.

He got a job. Nothing glamorous. Night janitor at an office building in midtown. Minimum wage. No benefits. No questions about his past.

He was invisible. Anonymous. Nothing.

He'd been King of 118th Street. Now he was nobody.

And that was freedom, in its own fucked up way.

Three months after the massacre, D Roc went back to 118th Street one last time.

Middle of the night. Nobody around. Just empty streets and streetlights and the memory of blood.

He walked the block slowly. End to end. Remembering.

This was where Peezy died. This was where Tone's body fell. This was where the building collapsed. This was where he killed Carmen.

Every inch of pavement held a ghost.

He found the stoop where he used to sit. Where he used to hold court. Where the corner boys used to come for their re-ups and the old heads used to nod their respect.

The building behind it was condemned now. Boarded up. Scheduled for demolition.

But the stoop was still there. Concrete and brick. Survivors.

D Roc sat down. Pulled out his last Newport. Lit it. Took a long drag.

Looked at his kingdom.

His block. His territory. His crown.

Empty. Destroyed. Worthless.

He'd killed everyone who tried to take it. Burned everything to keep it. Sacrificed everyone he loved to defend it.

And now?

Now it was his. All his. Nobody left to fight him for it.

King of 118th Street.

King of ashes. King of ghosts. King of Nothing.

He sat there smoking, watching the sun come up over the ruins of everything he'd built.

Somewhere in the city, Tasha was pregnant with his child. Somewhere, life continued without him. Somewhere, the world kept spinning like none of this ever mattered.

And maybe it didn't.

Maybe he'd fought a war over nothing. Killed for nothing. Died—in every way that mattered—for nothing.

King of Nothing.

But at least he was king.

At least he'd gone down swinging.

At least nobody owned him when the dust settled.

D Roc finished his cigarette. Crushed it under his Timbs. Looked at the empty block one more time.

Then he stood up.

Walked away.

And never came back.

CHAPTER TWENTY: KING OF NOTHING

Eight months later.

D Roc stood at the end of 118th Street, watching.

The block had changed. New buildings going up where the old ones burned. Fresh paint on the ones that survived. No more bullet holes in the brick. No more blood stains on the concrete. The city had scrubbed it clean, like none of it ever happened.

Like thirty-seven people didn't die here.

Like D Roc's kingdom didn't burn to ash on a Friday night in November.

It was July now. Hot. Summer thick in the air. Kids playing in open hydrants. Old ladies on stoops fanning themselves with church programs. The block was alive again. Different faces. New people who didn't know the history. Who didn't know what this pavement cost.

D Roc pulled his fitted cap lower. Different clothes now. Faded jeans. Plain white tee. No chains. No gun. Just another broke nigga walking through Harlem trying not to be seen.

Nobody recognized him. He'd lost weight—twenty pounds at least. The stress, the wounds, the cheap food. His face was harder now. Older. The kind of old that don't come from years but from seeing too much death.

He walked the block slowly. Past the spot where Peezy died—now a bodega with colorful awnings. Past where the building collapsed—now a construction site, steel beams reaching for the sky. Past where he killed Carmen—now just empty pavement where somebody left a teddy bear memorial for someone else's tragedy.

Everything was different. Everything was the same.

He reached the stoop. His stoop. The one where he used to hold court. Where he used to be King.

The building behind it was gone—torn down three months ago according to the notice he'd seen online. But the stoop remained. Concrete steps leading to nothing. A throne without a kingdom.

D Roc sat down. Pulled out a pack of Newports. His hands didn't shake anymore. Hadn't shaken in months. Whatever fear or adrenaline or humanity that used to make them shake was gone now.

He lit a cigarette. Took a drag. Watched the block live without him.

The night shift at the office building paid $15 an hour. He worked six nights a week. Lived in a basement studio in Washington Heights that cost too much and had roaches that didn't pay rent. Ate dollar pizza and bodega sandwiches. Sent money orders to a PO Box in New Jersey—Tasha's aunt's address. Never signed them. Never included a note. Just money. Three hundred dollars every two weeks.

For the baby.

His son.

He'd seen the birth announcement on Facebook. Tasha's page wasn't private. Maybe she didn't think he'd look. Maybe she didn't care.

Marcus Tone Freeman. Born March 17th. 7 lbs 3 oz. Healthy and perfect.

Marcus. After the kid who burned. Tone. After his brother who died calling for help.

His son carried the names of ghosts.

D Roc had stared at that photo for an hour. A tiny brown face, eyes closed, wrapped in a blue blanket. His son. His blood. A piece of him that existed in the world.

And he'd never hold him. Never teach him to tie his shoes or ride a bike or be a man. Never tell him stories or pass down wisdom or warn him about the streets.

Because the best thing D Roc could do for that boy was stay dead.

Stay a ghost.

Let him grow up thinking his father was a cautionary tale. A story mothers told to scare their kids straight.

Don't end up like D Roc. Don't let the streets swallow you. Don't become King of Nothing.

A kid on a bike rode past. Maybe twelve. Looked at D Roc sitting on the stoop, frowned like something was familiar but couldn't place it.

"This your spot?" the kid asked.

"Used to be."

"Well it ain't no more. This is Little Mike's block now. He run things here."

D Roc smiled. Bitter. "Little Mike, huh? He from around here?"

"Nah. From the Bronx. Moved in after... after what happened. You know. The war."

"I heard about that."

"My uncle died in that shit. He was just walking home from work. Caught a stray bullet." The kid's eyes were hard. Old. "They say it was some nigga named D Roc who started it. Say he called everybody to the block and got them all killed. Say he was crazy. Say he destroyed everything."

D Roc took a long drag. Let the smoke burn his lungs. "They say what happened to him?"

"Dead probably. Or locked up. Or hiding somewhere like a bitch." The kid spat. "Hope he dead though. Hope he died slow. He killed my uncle. Killed a lot of people's family."

"Yeah." D Roc's voice was quiet. "He did."

The kid rode away. D Roc sat there smoking, carrying the weight of that hate. The weight of being the villain in someone else's story. The monster who destroyed lives and didn't have the decency to die for it.

Another kid walked past. Different from the first. Twelve, maybe thirteen. Wearing a gold chain too big for his neck—the kind of chain an older brother might've owned. The kind Baby Face used to wear.

D Roc watched him walk by, shoulders hunched, eyes hard, trying to look tough even though he was just a baby. A baby who'd probably grow up hearing how his brother died in a shootout on 118th Street. A baby who'd probably never know his brother stayed because he didn't want to be seen as a coward. Who died so a twelve-year-old could inherit a chain and a legend and nothing else.

Detective Morrison never found him. The warrant was still active but the trail was cold. Without evidence, without witnesses, without any way to prove D Roc started the war, Morrison had nothing. The case went cold. Filed away with all the other unsolved murders that Harlem produced every year.

The media called it gang warfare. Cartel violence. The inevitable result of drugs and poverty and young men with guns and no future. They did special reports. Town halls. Community meetings about stopping the violence.

But they didn't understand. Couldn't understand. Because the violence wasn't random. Wasn't senseless. It was calculated. Strategic. The logical conclusion of every choice D Roc made since the first time he picked up a package and decided this life was worth living.

And now?

Now he was invisible. A ghost haunting the city that birthed him. Working for minimum wage. Living in a roach-infested basement. Sending money to a son who'd never know his name.

This was freedom.

This was winning.

This was what King looked like when the crown fell off and nobody bothered to pick it up.

The sun was setting. Orange and red painting the sky the color of fire. The color of that Friday night eight months ago.

D Roc finished his cigarette. Lit another. Last one in the pack. He made it last. Slow drags. Letting the nicotine settle in his blood like an old friend.

A woman walked by. Thirties. Dressed for work. Scrubs—probably a nurse. She glanced at him, kept walking, pulled her phone out like she was calling someone. Probably the cops. Strange man sitting on a stoop of a demolished building looked like trouble.

He didn't blame her. He was trouble. Had always been trouble. Would always be trouble.

Even when he was trying to be nothing.

Then he saw her.

Ms. Johnson. Lil Marcus's mama. Walking out of the corner bodega with a plastic bag, moving slow, looking older than her years. Grief had carved her face into something hard and hollow.

D Roc froze. Couldn't breathe. Couldn't move.

She looked up. Saw him. Stopped.

For a long moment, they just stared at each other. The woman whose son had burned alive because of him. The man who'd let it happen.

D Roc waited for her to scream. To curse him. To call him the devil like she had that day in her apartment. He deserved it. Deserved worse.

But she didn't scream.

She walked toward him. Slow. Deliberate. Stopped three feet away.

"I know who you are," she said quietly. "Even looking like that. I know."

"Yes ma'am."

"I prayed for you to die. Every night for months. Prayed God would strike you down for what you did to my baby."

D Roc nodded. "I'd have deserved it."

"You would have." She studied him with those ancient eyes. "But you didn't die. You're still here. Still breathing." She paused. "Why?"

"I don't know."

"Neither do I." Ms. Johnson shifted her grocery bag. "I stopped praying for your death three months ago. You know what I pray for now?"

"No ma'am."

"I pray you do something with the life my boy didn't get to live. I pray you find redemption, even if you don't deserve it. I pray you remember Marcus every single day and let that memory make you better."

D Roc's eyes burned. "I remember him. Every day."

"Good." She touched his cheek—the same way she had that day in her apartment, when she'd kissed his forehead like he was her own son. "Then don't waste it. Don't let his death mean nothing."

She walked away without looking back.

D Roc watched her go, feeling something crack open in his chest that had been sealed shut for months. Not forgiveness—he'd never deserve that. But permission. Permission to keep living. Permission to try to be something other than what he'd been.

The streetlights came on. One by one. Humming their electric song. The block settled into evening. Kids called inside for dinner. Cars cruising slow with music thumping. Life continuing like it always did. Like it always would.

Without him.

D Roc stood up. Bones creaking. Eight months of hard labor and cheap living had aged him. He felt forty though he wasn't even thirty yet.

He looked at the block one last time. His block. His territory. His kingdom.

New people running it now. Little Mike from the Bronx. Someone else's crew. Someone else's dream of being King.

They'd fall too. Eventually. The streets ate everyone. It was just a matter of time.

But that wasn't D Roc's problem anymore. He'd played the game. Made his moves. Won his war.

And lost everything that mattered.

Carmen was dead. Rodrigo was dead. Bishop and Trey were dead. Everyone who'd tried to own him or kill him or take what was his—all dead. All gone.

He'd won.

He was free.

He was King.

He looked at the empty stoop. At the demolished building. At the block that forgot him in less than a year.

Thought about Tone bleeding out on a basketball court. About Peezy shot twenty-three times for a bounty. About Lil Marcus burning alive. About all the bodies he'd stacked to keep this crown.

Thought about Tasha raising their son alone. Teaching him to hate the name D Roc. Teaching him that violence only breeds more violence. Teaching him to be better than his father ever was.

Thought about the kid on the bike whose uncle died in the crossfire. About the grandmother Marcus talked about who got killed trying to get to her apartment. About all the collateral damage that came with being King.

D Roc crushed his cigarette under his boot. The same Timbs he'd worn that night. Couldn't afford new ones. Couldn't afford much of anything.

He was King of 118th Street. King of Harlem. King of a territory nobody contested anymore because there was nothing left to contest.

He'd won his war. Stood alone at the end. Defeated everyone who came for him.

But standing here now, looking at his kingdom, D Roc realized the truth.

The crown was heavy. The throne was cold. The kingdom was ashes.

And he was alone.

No crew. No family. No woman. No son. No respect. No money. No future.

Nothing.

He'd killed everyone who tried to take it from him. Burned everything to keep it. Sacrificed everything he loved to protect it.

And in the end, he was King.

King of an empty block.

King of dead memories.

King of a war nobody won.

A slow smile spread across D Roc's face. Not happy. Not sad. Just accepting. Understanding. Finally seeing what he'd been too blind to see before.

"I guess I'm king now," he said to the empty street. To the ghosts that haunted every corner. To the version of himself that died here eight months ago.

He looked at the demolished building. At the rebuilt block. At the new faces living his old dream.

Looked at everything he'd won.

Everything he'd lost.

Everything he'd become.

"But King of what?" he whispered.

The words hung in the humid summer air. Truth distilled to its purest form. The answer he'd been running from since the first time someone called him King.

D Roc turned and walked away from 118th Street.

Away from his kingdom.

Away from his crown.

Away from everything he'd killed to protect.

And as he walked, the answer followed him like a shadow. Like a ghost. Like the truth that had been waiting all along.

* * *

Two weeks later, he took the train to Brooklyn.

Cypress Hills Cemetery had a small office near the gate where a tired-looking man in glasses asked him for a name. D Roc said it. Antoine Marcus Williams. Then he gave the date of birth and the date of death and watched the man write the plot number down on a piece of scrap paper without looking up.

Section 47. Row 12.

He walked it in the late afternoon light. Past granite angels and weeping mothers. Past the old graves with photographs in oval frames. Past the rows of veterans with flat brass markers. He walked slow, the way you walk when you don't want to get where you're going.

Tone's stone was small. Black granite, white letters. Just the name and the dates and *BELOVED SON AND BROTHER*. Ms. Gloria had paid for it. D Roc would have paid for something better, but he hadn't been welcome at the funeral and he hadn't been welcome to help.

He stood at the foot of the grave and didn't know what to do with his hands.

"It's me," he said finally. Quiet. Like he was afraid somebody would hear.

The wind moved through the trees. Somewhere above him, a crow called.

"I been by Peezy first. Mount Olive, out in Queens. They put him next to his cousin Reuben—you remember Reuben, got killed in the projects when we was twelve. Peezy used to tell stories about him. He's gonna talk that boy's ear off down there." He tried to laugh and it came out wrong. "He always did talk too much."

He sat down. Cross-legged on the grass, the way they used to sit on the basketball court at St. Nick's when they were kids and the world was small.

"I came to tell you I got a son. Marcus Tone Freeman. He got your name in the middle. Tasha picked it. She didn't ask me but she didn't have to."

He swallowed.

"I ain't gonna meet him. That's the deal I made with myself. Stay dead. Let him grow up not knowing who his daddy was. It's the only thing I can give him that ain't gonna get him killed."

He pulled the pack of Newports out of his pocket. Looked at it. Put it back without lighting one. Tone had always been on him about quitting.

"You was right, man. About all of it. About Bishop. About me getting too far in. About Carmen—you didn't even know her name yet and you was right." His eyes burned. "You was the smart one. I was the loud one. Nobody never noticed which was which because I was always making more noise. But you was the smart one. You always was."

He pulled something else out of his pocket. A postcard, soft at the corners from being handled too much. The front of it showed a pier in Boston, gulls in the sky. The back had a Massachusetts postmark from May and four lines in a young man's handwriting.

Mr. D Roc — I started college. Suffolk University. My abuela is good. She prays for you on Sundays even though I told her not to. I work at a bookstore in Back Bay. The boss doesn't know my real story. Nobody here does. Thank you for that. — M.R.

D Roc had read it more times than he could count. He hadn't written back. There was no return address. Marcus was smart enough not to leave one.

"This kid I told you about. The one Carmen wanted me to do, the college boy in Washington Heights." He held the postcard like it might break. "He's in Boston. Got into a school. Got a job at a bookstore. I told myself when I let him go that night that maybe one good thing was enough. I didn't believe it. But here it is. He wrote me." He laughed, and it was the first sound that resembled a laugh he'd made in months. "Kid wrote me a thank-you card, T. Like I did something nice. Like I wasn't sent there to put him in the ground."

He put the postcard back in his pocket. Carefully. Like it was the only thing in his life that was still worth anything.

"Maybe that's the math. Maybe one is what I get. One name on the right side of the column." He shook his head. "It ain't enough. I know it ain't enough. Ms. Johnson's boy is still dead. You still dead. Peezy still dead. But it's something. It's the only something I got."

He stayed until the sun went down behind the trees and the air turned cool. The cemetery had a curfew but nobody came to chase him out. Maybe they saw him sitting there and figured he had a right.

When he finally stood up, his knees popped.

"I'm gonna do something with what's left, T. I don't know what yet. I been thinking maybe one of them programs—the ones at St. Nick's, with the kids. Just listening. Just being one more person who tells them not to do what I did. I don't know if they'd let me. Probably not. But I'm gonna ask."

He pressed his palm flat against the top of the stone. The granite was cool even in the July heat.

"I love you. I'm sorry."

He walked out the way he came. Two trains and a bus back to Washington Heights. Didn't smoke the whole way home.

* * *

Three weeks later.

D Roc stood across the street from St. Nicholas Park, hidden in the shadow of a bodega awning, watching.

Tasha sat on a bench near the playground, a stroller beside her. She looked different—softer somehow, less guarded. Motherhood had changed her in ways D Roc couldn't name but could see from fifty feet away.

The baby was awake. He could tell by the way Tasha leaned into the stroller, cooing, making faces. Then she lifted him out—a small brown bundle in a blue onesie—and held him against her chest.

Marcus Tone Freeman. Named for ghosts.

D Roc's son.

He watched them for twenty minutes. Watched Tasha walk the baby around, pointing at birds and squirrels. Watched her sit back down and feed him from a bottle. Watched her laugh at something the baby did—his first smile maybe, or just gas. Either way, she looked happier than D Roc had ever seen her.

Happier without him.

He wanted to cross the street. Wanted to hold his son just once. Feel that weight in his arms. See if the boy had his eyes or Tasha's. Tell him something—anything—that might matter someday.

But he didn't move.

Because the best thing he could give his son was his absence. The best legacy he could leave was being a story Tasha told to keep him straight: *Don't end up like your father. Don't let the streets swallow you whole.*

King of Nothing.

Not even king of his own child's memory.

Tasha looked up suddenly, scanning the street like she felt someone watching. D Roc stepped back into the shadow, held his breath. Her eyes passed over him without recognition. He was just another stranger now. Another ghost on a Harlem corner.

She turned back to the baby.

D Roc watched for one more minute. Memorizing. The curve of his son's cheek. The way Tasha held him like he was made of something precious. The life they would have without him.

Then he turned and walked away.

Didn't look back.

Couldn't.

His hand went to his pocket—the old habit, reaching for a Newport. But the pack was empty. Had been for three days. He hadn't bought more.

Maybe that was something. Maybe that was a start.

Some crowns you wear.

Some crowns you bury.

And some crowns were never yours to begin with.

But maybe—just maybe—a father of something. Even if that something was just a prayer his son would never have to wear the same crown.

The End.

ABOUT THE AUTHOR

Lampert x Griffin Urban Universe™ creates urban fiction that captures the raw reality of street life while delivering powerful messages through consequence rather than preaching.

King of Nothing is the first novel in the Lampert x Griffin Urban Universe™.

For updates on future releases, follow Lampert x Griffin Urban Universe™.

www.ingramcontent.com/pod-product-compliance
Lightning Source LLC
LaVergne TN
LVHW010703110826
845149LV00014B/3208